The Bat Riders of Yumi

Matthew John sounds the horn of Anoura and takes to the air with all of the bat rider squadrons of Yumi to save his parents and his friends from a forest fire.

The Bat Rider Books

Bat Rider

On the planet of the mile-high Yumi trees, only a few lucky boys and girls may fly bats to the treetops to harvest the fruit. Matthew John would like to join them, but to make his dream come true he must enter the cave of Oomba the lion.

*'My kids would not put out the light
until we had finished the book.'*

-- Singaporean Reviewer

Bat Rider is available in print and as an e-book from

Amazon.com

The Yumi Trees

The mile-high Yumi trees are in danger and Matthew John wishes to save them.
His mission takes him to the Black Sun, Kanji Island and the Enchanted Grove.
Every day Matthew John grows older and bigger.
What if he grows too big to ride his bat?

*'It's really imaginative and adventurous – almost like one
of those dreams you don't like to wake up from.'*

-- Canadian reviewer

The Yumi Trees is available in print and as an e-book from

Amazon.com

ANTHONY BARTON

The Bat Riders of Yumi

WITH DECORATIONS BY THE AUTHOR

Bulmer Press

THE BAT RIDERS OF YUMI

Bulmer Press Edition
Copyright © 2012 Anthony Barton
Library and Archives Canada Cataloguing in Publication
Barton, Anthony, 1942-
The Bat Riders of Yumi / Anthony Barton; with decorations by the author.
ISBN 978-0-9878454-5-0
I. Title.
PS8553.A7776B39 2012 jC813'.6 C2012-902839-8
Cover and drawings by Anthony Barton. All Rights Reserved.

TO THE BATS OF THE WORLD

Matthew John and I
wish you happy flying
for years to come
with all our love

Contents

CHAPTER I

Saying Hello to Pudding

I CAN SEE the glowing moss of the cave reflected in the eyes of the bats.

'This is Pudding,' I say, putting Matthew John's stuffed toy bat down on the cave floor.

'Hello, Pudding.' The bats crowd around to have a closer look.

'His vings zey are too small,' says Lara, the bat from Number Eight Squadron.

'With wings like that, he'd better not try to fly,' says Pinky.

'He did try to fly once,' I say. 'Matthew John's mother gave him a good wash and hung him up to dry on her clothesline. A hot wind sprang up, and Pudding let go of the line.'

'What happened?' asks Hula.

'He was carried away by the wind.'

'And?' says Hula.

The bats look at me eagerly, their eyes bright.

'He saved Matthew John's life.'

'Pudding saved Matthew John's *life*?' says Pinky, breathlessly.

'Ve vant to hear whole story,' says Lara.

'I'd better begin at the beginning then. The tale begins in a city filled with ghosts,' I say. 'Is anyone here frightened of ghosts?'

The bats look at me, their eyes wide.

'Does Matthew John's bat Bulmer come into the story?' asks Hula, trying to remember.

'Yes, he does,' I say. 'He turns into a ghost. Shall I begin?'

'Yes, please,' says Hula.

The bats lean forward to listen.

THE BAT RIDERS OF YUMI

CHAPTER II

Bulmer the Ghost

'WE ARE ENTERING the atmosphere,' said Matthew John, speaking to his mother on his Bat Rider phone.

'Have you really found the ancient city of Chiroptera?' she asked.

'We can see the tumbled remains. We're trying to land as close to the ruins as possible.'

'Are you sure its safe?' she said. 'Your father wants a word with you.'

'Dad? Is that you?'

'When you are full of dread, keep your head,' said his father.

'Thanks, Dad.'

'Mr. Seeds warns you not to eat any ghost food. He tells me you may have a chance to free the lost squadron of Anoura.'

'Did he say Anoura?' asked Matthew John frowned. 'Anoura, the legendary first Bat Rider?'

'We've hit the Heaviside Layer, captain,' said the helmsman.

'I'm picking up evidence of non-corporeal life,' said the science officer.

'Non-corporeal?' said Matthew John.

'I can see something off our starboard bow. It is definitely a ghost. The planet must be haunted.'

'We are losing voice and visual.'

The screen went blank.

'Dad? Mum? Are you there?'

No answer.

'Can you hear anything, Bulmer?'

Bulmer cocked his head and pricked his ears. Bats have sensitive hearing. 'I hear ghosts wailing,' he said.

'Take her in,' ordered Matthew John.

The starship Artibeus dived through a cloud of ectoplasm, bounced off the Great Beyond, and landed heavily in an alien graveyard, knocking over a sarcophagus. Ghastly laughter echoed through the ship. Strange blue lights flickered, and things made of bones danced among the leaning stones.

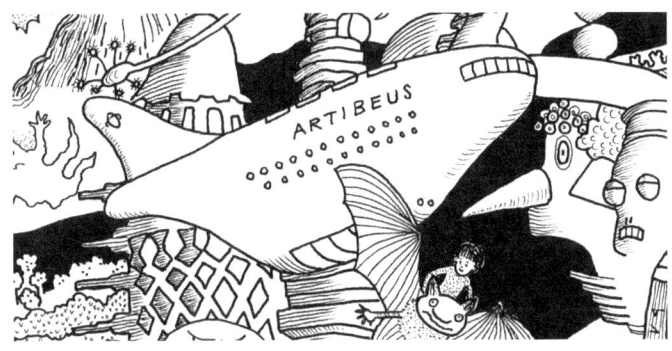

'Our mission is to brave the ghosts of Chiroptera and find the lost squadron of Anoura,' said Matthew John. 'Who would like to come?'

'Sounds interesting,' said Joshua Ryan.

'Dangerous, too,' said Annabelle Sue.

Emily Charlotte cleared her throat.

'I hope *you* are not going to volunteer,' said her bat Vesper.

'Of course I'm going to volunteer,' replied Emily Charlotte, 'and my brother, Joshua Ryan, is, too. Aren't you, brother of mine?' She dug an elbow into his ribs.

'A chance to explore the ancient city of Chiroptera?' said Joshua Ryan. 'A chance to discover the truth about Anoura and her Wild Ride? I wouldn't miss it for the world.'

'Count me in, too,' said Annabelle Sue. 'My bat Hula loves alien graveyards, don't you, Hula?'

'I s-suppose so,' said Hula.

'Don't worry, Hula,' said Vesper. 'If you turn into a ghost, you won't feel a thing. That's a joke. Ghosts don't feel anything. And you thought I didn't have a sense of fun.'

'Open the airlock!' said Matthew John.

Matthew John and his three volunteers flew low over the tumbled buildings of the ancient city. High levels of oxygen and weak gravity made it easy for their bats to bear their weight.

They dived beneath a buttress of translucent stone and hovered over a winged memorial.

Matthew John thought he spied a creature out of the corner of his eye. The beast darted out of sight among the shadows before he had a chance to see what it was.

A puff of air ruffled Matthew John's hair.

A horn sounded far away amid the ruined spires.

'Warooo!' said the horn.

'Did you hear that?' asked Annabelle Sue, her eyes bright with excitement. 'Someone knows we're here.'

'This is an abandoned city,' said Joshua Ryan, frowning. 'There should be *nobody* here.'

'But there *is* somebody,' said Emily Charlotte, craning her neck. 'Look over there! I can see a light.'

She pointed up at a glowing doorway.

'She's right about the light,' said Bulmer.

'Follow me!' said Matthew John. He flew his bat Bulmer through the shining doorway. 'I see a king sitting on a throne. Uh-oh! The king has no head.'

Matthew John flew into a spacious dining hall.

His friends followed.

'Wizzo!' said Bulmer. 'They've laid on a bang-up feast.'

'Who are "they"?' asked Emily Charlotte.

'Just the right number of chairs to seat eight guests,' said Matthew John, thoughtfully, staring down at a table weighed down with food and steaming cocoa. He could see dishes heaped with octopus burgers, marshmallow sandwiches and peanut butter turtles.

At the head of the table sat the headless king.

'Welcome!' said a voice issuing from the darkness where the head should have been. 'I am King Mimon, ruler of Chiroptera. I have had this special meal prepared for you. Be seated, visitors from the starship Artibeus. Help yourselves. Have some spooky soup. May I pour you a glass of ghostly wine? What brings you to my ancient city?'

Of the eight chairs arranged around the table for the visitors, four were built for bats and four were built for humans. Matthew John chose a chair built for humans next to the headless King, while Bulmer hung himself upside in one of the chairs built for bats. The others seated themselves elsewhere around the shimmering table, and eyed the strange ghostly dishes set before them.

Matthew John whispered in Bulmer's ear. 'Remember what Mr. Seeds said. Don't eat any of the ghost food or you'll turn into a ghost.'

Bulmer's eyes widened. He did not want to turn

into a ghost. Yet the peanut butter turtles looked yummy. His tummy rumbled. 'Mmm,' he said to himself. 'Maybe just a little biddy one? Just to see how it tastes?' He reached out with a claw to help himself.

'We have come in search of Anoura and her lost squadron of bat riders,' said Matthew John to the headless King. Matthew John took a ghostly octopus burger from a dish and held it in front of his mouth. He pretended to bite into it. He wanted the headless king to think he was enjoying the ghost food. He did not let the burger touch his lips.

'Did you say Anoura?' cried King Mimon, waving his arms excitedly. 'You are searching for my sister?'

Lightning lit up the sky and a crash of thunder rumbled over the ruined city.

'Wow!' said Annabelle Sue. 'That thing with the thunder. You can do that by waving your arms?'

King Mimon shrugged his shoulders. 'My head makes the thunder and lightning,' he said. 'Not me.'

'But you don't have a head,' said Joshua Ryan, tactlessly.

'Actually, I do have a head,' the king replied, 'but it is not attached to my body at the moment. I lost my head one day when I was experimenting in my weather laboratory.'

'Your head is... somewhere else?' asked Emily Charlotte.

'My head is up in the sky stirring up the clouds. Judging by the noise, I should say that the mention of Anoura's name has made my head angry. You see, many years ago Anoura entered my laboratory at just the wrong moment...

"You had better be careful," Anoura said, and, like a fool, I took my eye off my lightning machine to frown at her, and the next thing I knew, the lightning machine had blown my head off. I felt pretty stupid without a head, let me tell you.'

'What is it like to be without a head?' asked Joshua Ryan.

'It's disconcerting,' replied the king. 'Anoura and I never got along very well even when we were children. My sister would not let me play with her bats.' The king clenched his fists. 'Aurora taught her bats to do the most wonderful tricks. Her bats would do anything for her. They would loop the loop, they would fly though a hoop, they would even let my sister ride on their backs. When I saw Anoura playing with her bats, I grew jealous. The day I spied her gliding among the huge tree trunks of the ancient forest, seated upon the neck of her greatest friend and companion, the mighty Bat himself, with that self-satisfied smile of hers on her lips, that was the final straw. I couldn't bear it anymore. Something inside me snapped.

"Let me ride a bat too, Anoura!' I begged. "Let me join your Wild Ride."

"Never, Mimon," she replied. "Your head is stuffed with thunder and lightning. You would scare my bats. Girls may ride bats, but not boys, not until the day a boy rides in here on the back of his very own bat."

Anoura raised her left arm so that the golden light of the setting sun flashed from her silver bracelet depicting Ia the Great Bat of Evening.

'At her signal, twenty girls rode out of the mist, all mounted on bats. Anoura's Wild Ride had begun, but I had been left out. There was no bat for me to ride.'

King Mimon slumped in his chair.

'So what did you do?' asked Matthew John. He found it hard to read the thoughts of a person whose face was not there.

'I'll tell you what I did,' said the king. 'I vowed that if I could not ride, then my sister and her friends would not ride either. Thunderbolts crackled and spat. The heavens roared…'

'It was you!' cried Annabelle Sue, jumping to her feet and throwing her ghostly marshmallow sandwich on the table. 'It was you who brought the towers down. It was you who destroyed the beautiful city of Chiroptera. It was you who imprisoned your sister.'

'No, no,' said the headless King. 'You don't understand. My *head* brought down the city, not me.'

'I don't care who did it, you or your stupid head,' said Annabelle Sue. 'It was terrible to bring a whole city to ruin just to spite your sister.'

'What became of your sister and her riders?' asked Joshua Ryan, always practical. 'Did they die when you destroyed the city?'

King Mimon did not answer. He began to fade.

Matthew John could see through the king's hands. As the king faded, so did his chair and table. The peanut butter turtles became transparent. The other dishes on the table grew dim and then winked out of existence. The green light went out, plunging Matthew John and his friends into darkness. The chairs vanished and Matthew John found himself sprawled on the floor. He felt about and touched something furry. 'Bulmer, is that you?'

'I think so,' said Bulmer, but his voice sounded as if he were speaking from another world.

Then, for the second time, a horn sounded.

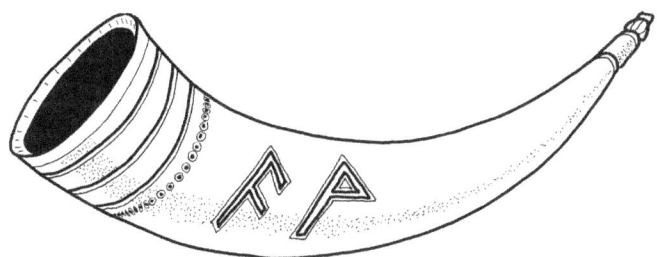

'Warooo!' said the horn.

'Who is blowing that horn?' said Matthew John. 'I hope it is Anoura. I hope she survived the fall of the city.'

Anoura, the first person ever to ride a bat, was resting her Wild Riders' Horn on her chest as she lay back in her casket. 'I felt him close by, the Boy with the Bat,' she said to herself. 'He must be near. Why can't I see him? Why can't he see me? Great squeaking vampires! Now that I have sounded the horn for the second time, I feel exhausted. I wonder why I am lying in this casket?'

She sat up in a hurry and wiped a cobweb from her face. 'How long have I been asleep?' She stared about her in dismay. She was in a crypt. The crypt had a vaulted ceiling. Her stone casket lay in the middle of the crypt. All around, arranged in a circle, lay twenty other similar caskets.

She scrambled to her feet. She jumped out of her casket and laid the Wild Riders' Horn carefully on the flagstone floor. She brushed dust from her arms and legs and ran to look inside another casket. She saw a girl there, covered by a thick layer of dust. She blew the dust from the girl's face. 'Tut Nut?'

'Tut Nut, wake up!' she said, grabbing the girl by the shoulders and giving her a good shake. 'We have to find our bats. Didn't you hear me blow the horn?'

'Wassamatta?' said Tut Nut, sleepily.

'Sizzling zombies!' said Anoura. 'Wake up, Tut Nut! We've been entranced.'

Anoura ran from casket to casket, waking her sleeping riders. Soon all of her twenty companions were out of their caskets and slapping dust from one another's backs.

'Where's Noctilio?' said a newly awakened girl called Pana Rana, running this way and that, searching for her bat. 'Noctilio! Are you there? Noctilio?'

'I think I heard him squeak,' said Pana Rama. 'I think I heard my bat Noctilo squeak. He must be trapped behind this wall. All of our bats must be.'

Noctilio squeaked again.

This time all the girls heard him.

'Sounds like you are right, Pana Rana,' said Anoura, and ran her hands over a sculpted relief on the wall depicting winged creatures. 'Galloping ghouls! I can feel ancient letters carved in the stone.'

The girls ran to her side.

They explored a dozen nooks and crannies in the wall, looking for a secret lever.

Then Tut Nut traced the symbols with her fingers and said 'The runes are carved in the language of ancient Chiroptera. They say:

ONE FOR THE MASTER, ONE FOR THE MAID, AND ONE FOR THE CRYPT WHERE THE BATS ARE LAID

'Groaning goblins!' said Anoura. 'A message from the day the city fell.'

30

'It sounds like a riddle,' said Pana Rana. 'Perhaps we have to figure out the answer.'

'If only the Boy with the Bat were here to help us,' said Anoura.

On the far side of the city, the Boy with the Bat was feeling for his bat's wings.

Bulmer felt a bit strange. He could not see his feet.

'Keep still, Bulmer, I am trying to climb onto your back.' Matthew John found the bat's neck at last and seated himself. He dug his hands into Bulmer's fur. 'Is everybody ready to fly?' he asked.

'All set,' said Joshua Ryan, who had made himself comfortable on the back of his own bat Smoky.

'Ready,' said his sister Emily Charlotte, who had mounted her bat Vesper.

'I'm in the air already,' said Annabelle Sue, who was never one to wait for orders. 'Hula wants to know which way to fly.'

'We must find the person who blew that horn,' said Matthew John, and flew his bat Bulmer out through a shattered window of the ruined spire. 'Head for the heart of Chiroptera!'

'Matthew John!' cried Emily Charlotte. 'Where's your bat?'

Matthew John frowned. 'Don't be silly. I'm riding my… ' He looked down.

There was nothing between his knees. He could see straight down to the city below.

'Bulmer? Where have you gone?'

A faint throaty whisper answered 'I can't see my wings or my feet.'

'Bulmer, did you eat the ghost food?'

'No. I mean yes. Well, uh, just a little bit,' said Bulmer's whispery voice. 'A couple of peanut butter turtles and thirty-six marshmallow sandwiches. The marshmallow sandwiches were really good.'

Matthew John sighed. 'Oh, Bulmer,' he said. 'I warned you. Now you're a ghost.'

'Me?' said Bulmer. 'A ghost? Are you sure?'

'I can't see you, Bulmer,' said Matthew John. 'I'm riding an invisible bat.'

'Oh, boy,' said Bulmer. 'Then I must be a ghost. Is that why that ghost crab down there is waving its pincers at me?'

'I can't see the ghost crab,' said Matthew John, 'but perhaps, now that you're a ghost yourself, you can see other ghosts more easily than I can. Perhaps this ghost crab of yours knows who is sounding the horn. Take us down, Bulmer, and we'll ask the crab.'

They landed by the entrance to a catacomb. The passage was barred by an iron gate decorated with skulls.

'Say something, Bulmer. Talk to the ghost crab.'

'Hello ghost crab,' said Bulmer.

'I'm glad you have come to relieve me,' said the ghost crab, using his eight walking legs to run sideways while he scratched his carapace with his other two legs. 'It's not easy guarding the tomb of Anoura. I've been here so long I can't even remember the password. Let me see, was the password HAT BOY or was it CAT BOY?'

'Uh. How about BAT BOY,' suggested Bulmer.

The iron gate creaked open on rusty hinges and sepulchral voice said 'Welcome, Boy with the Bat, to the Tomb of Anoura.'

'Shivering specters!' said Anoura. 'Did you hear that creaking gate? The Boy with the Bat has come to rescue us, just as the ancient legend said he would. I feel his presence. He is near. Hurry! We must free our bats and be ready. But how do we free our bats?'

Anoura and her twenty riders stood and stared at the baffling runes on the wall, wondering how to free their bats. They were anxious to rescue their bats from the crypt in which the poor creatures had hung by their feet for centuries, dreaming their enchanted dreams.

'One for the master, say the runes' said Tut Nut. 'The ancient word for boy was "master" wasn't it?'

'Yes,' said Pana Rana. 'That would be the Boy on the Bat. And the ancient word for girl was…'

Anoura slapped her forehead with the flat of her hand. 'I've been a fool! The answer to the riddle is simple. The ancient word for girl was "maid." That must be me. *One for the master, one for the maid, and one for the crypt where the bats are laid.* I sounded the Wild Riders' Horn once when I felt the Boy with the Bat was near. I sounded the horn again to wake you girls from your enchanted sleep. Now I must sound the horn for a third time to liberate our bats. That is the answer to the riddle.'

Anoura lifted the horn to her lips, took a deep breath and sounded the horn.

'Warooo!' said the Wild Riders' horn for the third time.

Into the yawning tomb of Anoura flew Matthew John and his friends. Unseen fingers tugged at their hair. Something tottered towards them, half bat and half cow, trailing mummy bandages.

'Yikes!' said Bulmer.

'To the left,' said Matthew John, swerving in the air. It was hard to steer an invisible bat.

They veered beneath the flailing arms of the bat-cow zombie and shot into a tunnel full of banshees.

'Cover your ears!' said Emily Charlotte.

The bat riders covered their ears with their hands, gripping their bats extra tightly with their knees. The tunnel dipped and they swooped into a pit.

'Yay!' said Annabelle Sue, skimming low over the surface of lake of evil froth. A skeletal hand reached up from the lake and pinched her foot.

A moment later they were sucked up a shaft by a whirling zephyr and sent flailing into darkness. 'I can't see,' said Bulmer, flapping his invisible wings helplessly.

'Use echo-location!' said Matthew John. He had a deep-seated fear of the dark, and was glad he was riding a bat who could see in the dark better than he.

Even an invisible bat can see better in the dark than in the daylight, with the help of his ears.

'Eep! Eep!' said Bulmer, sending out high-pitched squeaks while rotating his sensitive ears to hear his squeaks bouncing back to him.

'Uh. I can see a thingy,' said Bulmer.

'What sort of a thing is it?'

'You don't want to know,' said Bulmer.

'Tell me.'

'A thingy that sucks blood,' said Bulmer.

'Oh, no!' said Vesper. 'Please don't let it be a vampire. Can we go home now? I really want to go home.'

'M-me, too,' said Hula.

'We must find Anoura first,' said Matthew John.

'We can't turn back now,' he went on. 'Twice Anoura's horn has sounded, so we know she needs our help. Fly on!'

So they flew on. They entered a haunted cavern. Scores of green glowing specters surrounded them, floating in the air. 'Go back! Go back!' they chorused. 'You can't come here. How dare you disturb Anoura the fair! Begone! Begone! Anoura and her bats sleep on, sleep on!'

'Twice we have heard Anoura's horn,' said Matthew John. 'She sleeps no more! Let us pass. Your long vigil is over.'

'You lie! You lie!' sang the green specters, pressing closer. 'She sleeps! She sleeps!'

'Warooo!' said the Wild Riders' horn for the third time, close at hand.

'The horn sounds again!' said Matthew John. 'Anoura is here!'

Anoura took the horn from her lips and stared at the runes incised on the stone. She saw a tiny crack in the middle of the runes that spelled the word WHERE. The crack widened and grew longer, splitting open the runes for MAID and then the runes for LAID.

A sudden silence gripped the city, as if the whole of Chiroptera held its breath. Then came a rolling thunder, not in the sky but deep underground, and Anoura felt the rock floor of the crypt heave beneath the soles of her feet.

'Step back!' she shouted. 'The wall may give way.'

The carved figures of winged creatures fell apart. The stones of the wall came tumbling down, dust filled the air, and a gaping hole revealed another, larger crypt beyond their own.

'Bat!' cried Anoura, leaping over the rubble of the ruined wall. 'Bat, are you there?'

Anoura climbed up a cobwebby rope and leaped onto a hanging walkway. She ran along narrow wooden slats. The gantry swayed as she ran, threatening to send her tumbling to the crypt floor below. 'Bat?' she said again.

She was wondering if her dear companion was still alive. It was dreadful to think that he might not have survived the long years of enchanted sleep.

The ropes of the walkway felt brittle under her fingers, and creaked ominously.

'Anoura?' said an uncertain voice from the darkness. 'Anoura, is that you?'

'Bat! You're alive!' Anoura flung herself on to the back of her good friend Bat, the first bat ever to fly with a human being on his back. She hugged Bat tightly, pressing her cheek into his soft fur. 'Poor old Bat,' she said, gently. He smelled of dust and bones.

'We have to escape from this awful tomb, Bat,' she went on.

Bat squeaked and cocked his ears. 'I can't see how we can,' he said. 'My ears tell me we are trapped inside a cave with no exit, and we have no way to leave.'

'Don't worry. The Boy with a Bat has come to free us,' said Anoura. 'I can feel him. He is very close.'

She raised her right arm. Her bracelet glowed with the radiant energy of Ia, the Great Bat of Evening, and she called out to her companions. 'Wild Riders! Have you all found your bats?'

Happy voices replied from all corners of the crypt.

'I have found Noctilio,' said Pana Rana. 'He is shaking the dust from his wings.'

'I have found Mystacina,' said Tut Nut. 'She is singing the praises of Ia.'

Twenty voices answered joyfully that their bats had been found. The Wild Ride was ready to take to the skies. But where was the Boy with the Bat who alone, according to legend, could break the spell and let Anoura and her Riders out if their underground prison? Where was Matthew John?

Matthew John was struggling to free himself from the mass of the green specters, but the specters would not let him go. They would not let him enter the inner sanctum of Anoura. 'You foolish specters!' he said, pushing them away as hard as he could. 'You heard the horn. The horn has sounded three times! Don't you remember the legend? I am the Boy with the Bat! Let me in! The hour has come for me to free Anoura and her Wild Riders.'

'Only ghosts may pass the threshold of Anoura's sepulcher,' said a specter, chuckling.

Another specter cackled: 'Only a ghost can free Anoura. Are you a ghost? I think not. You feel like flesh and blood to me, boy!'

Matthew John felt the specter's mouth gnaw at his hair. Icy cold shot through his skull.

'You are wrong,' said Matthew John. 'My bat is a ghost.'

The specters fell silent. They stared at the space between Matthew John's legs.

'How can your bat be a ghost?' said the first specter.

'Bulmer,' whispered Matthew John. 'Say something. Speak to me!'

'Uh,' said Bulmer. 'I ate the marshmallow sandwiches on the Headless King's table. I started to feel all wobbly, and then I could see though my wings. Now I can't see myself at all.'

'Say something *scary*,' whispered Matthew John. 'You're a ghost, remember?'

'Boo!' said Bulmer.

The specters fled in terror. 'Boo!' was the rudest word they knew.

'Quick!' said Matthew John the moment the specters were gone.

He urged Bulmer forward.

Matthew John and his friends swooped into the inner sanctum of Anoura.

'What's that up ahead?' asked Annabelle Sue.

'It looks like a head with no body,' said Joshua Ryan. 'The head seems to be floating in the dark. I can hear a crackling sound, and my hair is standing on end.'

'What are you doing down here in Anoura's tomb, head?' asked Emily Charlotte.

'I am the head of the King of Chiroptera,' said the head. 'Anoura entered my laboratory unannounced. There was an explosion. I was separated me from my body and I was flung into the heavens. But I took my revenge upon Anoura. I trapped her in this crypt. Only a Boy with a Bat may release her. You cannot be that Boy because you have no bat. So come no closer! I warn you, I am imbued with dreadful powers.'

A bolt of electricity shot out of the head and shattered a boulder beside Emily Charlotte. Thunder crashed and reverberated in the underground vault, making Matthew John's ears sing. Fragments of rock whizzed past Vesper's nose.

'I knew that coming to this city was a bad idea,' said Vesper, fanning her face with her wings. 'A mission to a City of Ghosts! I ask you. I shouldn't be surprised if we all lose our heads before we're through. Why don't we give up this whole business right now?'

'No,' said Matthew John. 'We can't leave until we have freed Anoura and her Wild Ride. That is our mission, if you recall.'

'Your mission has failed,' said the head. 'Go back to your ship!' The head's eyes turned red. A howling wind slammed the riders and their bats into the crypt walls.

'Ouch!' said Joshua Ryan's bat Smoky.

'Oof!' said Annabelle Sue.

'Wait! I see runes on these walls,' said Hula. 'Does anyone know what they mean?'

'It must be another puzzle,' said Joshua Ryan. 'The runes have a message for us.'

THREE LETTERS SPELL THE ANCIENT NAME
OF HE WHO SHARES ANOURA'S FAME

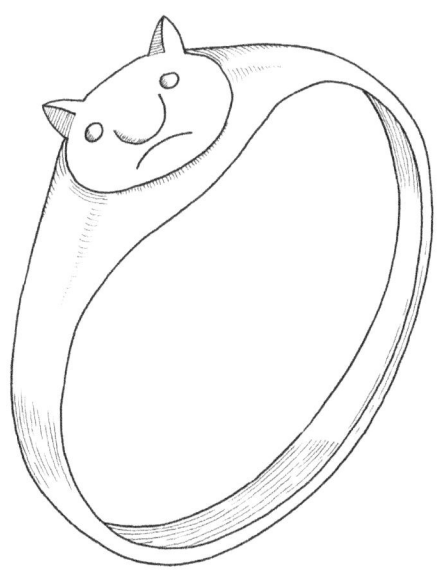

'What is the name of the Great Bat of Evening?' asked Matthew John. 'Can anyone remember?'

'Ia,' said Annabelle Sue. 'But Ia has only two letters.'

'You try my patience,' said the head, and puffed up its cheeks. 'Take this, you tomb robbers!' The head expelled a foul vapor.

'We're done for,' said Vesper. 'We're all going to die of bad breath.'

'Don't breathe in, whatever you do,' said Matthew John, holding his nose 'What ith the name of Anorath companion? I can't think thtraight.'

'I believe,' said Joshua Ryan, 'that Anoura's companion was called...'

'Uh. B – A – T has three letters,' said Bulmer.

'Bat!' said Matthew John. 'That's it! Bulmer, you've done it. The ancient name of Anoura's bat is Bat. Everybody yell "Bat." One, two, three…'

'BAT!' shouted the bat riders and their bats.

The runes cracked, the ground trembled, the wall caved in, and Anoura's Ride burst from their prison, trailing a cloud of dust.

'Warooo!' said the Wild Riders' horn for the fourth time.

'Fly with me!' cried Anoura, grabbing her brother's head by its hair.

Out of the vaults in which they had been held for centuries rose Anoura and her twenty Wild Riders, and Matthew John and his friends rose with them. They winged their way through long forgotten passages and ascended from the ruins of Chiroptera as dawn broke.

Again and again the horn sounded above the city. 'Warooo!' said the horn. 'Warooo! Warooo!'

'Mimon!' called Anoura. 'Come out, my brother. I have a gift for you.'

Out of the ruined weather experimental station stepped the headless king. 'What gift do you bring me, Anoura?' he cried, 'after all your years imprisoned in the crypt by that wicked head of mine?'

'I bring you your head,' she said, and she placed her brother's head back on his shoulders.

The moment the head was replaced, the curse was reversed, the spell overturned, and bright sunshine burst through the storm clouds. In the wink of an eye, the city was restored. The toppled spires became tall and straight once more. The ghosts and goblins crept no more, but stood up straight and walked, proud citizens of a proud city. The laughter of children rang once more in the streets of Chiroptera.

Matthew John saw merchants open their stalls, and heard bells peal cheerfully. The city lived again. He and his friends had succeeded in their mission. 'You did it, Bulmer,' he said, excitedly. 'You solved the riddle! I'm so proud of you!'

But when Matthew John looked down, his heart sank. 'Anoura!' he said. 'My bat is still a ghost.'

'So you are the Boy with the Bat?' said Anoura.

Matthew John nodded. He felt shy, and was not sure how to talk to the first human being ever to fly a bat, but his Bulmer was in trouble, so he had to beg her for help. 'Yes, my name's Matthew John. Is there anything you can do for my friend Bulmer?'

Bulmer ate the ghost food your brother laid before him, and now he can't see his own body, and I can't see him. It's a bit awkward. You see, we've been friends for years, Bulmer and I.'

'I'll lend you this,' said Anoura and placed in Matthew John's hands the Wild Riders' horn. 'I think my horn has a little power left in it. Enough to save your friend.'

'How can I thank you?' said Matthew John, gazing in wonder at the silver horn.

'It is I who should thank you, Matthew John, for you played your part. You woke us from our enchanted sleep. Your actions have helped restore the ancient city and have put life back into her people. For that, you deserve the loan of my horn. It is yours for as long as you need it. Guard it well, and if ever you find yourself in trouble, please sound the horn, and, wherever I may be, I shall hear it.'

Matthew John looked up and searched Anoura's face. 'Are you going to stay here to help your brother rule the city?' he asked.

Anoura shook her head. 'My brother and I don't get along.'

'Come with us on the Artibeus, then,' said Matthew John. 'We could do with your help.'

Anoura shook her head. 'Thank you, but I fear our long sleep has left my riders and myself too weak for that. We have barely enough strength to take off. Will you blow the horn one more time for us?'

Matthew John nodded. He drew a deep breath to fill his lungs, and then sounded the horn.

'Warooo!' went the horn.

Anoura and her twenty riders sprang into the air, borne aloft by the wings of their ancient bats. Higher and higher they flew.

Matthew John and his friends shaded their eyes against the setting sun, and followed their progress. The Wild Ride became tiny dots in the evening sky.

Faintly they heard twenty-one voices shout 'Ia!'

Anoura and her riders vanished among the clouds.

'Will we ever see them again?' asked Bulmer.

Matthew John took the horn from his lips and ran his fingertips over the fluting. 'We may see them again one day, if ever we need them,' he said, and scratched Bulmer on the top his head, which was his bat's favorite place for being scratched. 'But as long as I can see you, Bulmer, that's what really matters.'

'You *can* you see me?' asked Bulmer, surprised. 'I thought I was a ghost.'

'You are not a ghost any more,' said Matthew John. 'Look at your wings.'

'You're right. I'm me again. I can feel you scratching my head.' Bulmer grinned. 'I've got my head back, just like the king.'

An ominous rumble came from the sky. Lightning flickered among the spires of the resurrected city.

'I don't think the king is too happy about having his head back,' said Matthew John. 'Let's be quick about leaving.'

Matthew John strode onto the bridge of the Artibeus.

'Take us up, helm,' he said.

'Aye, aye, captain,' said the helmsman.

The starship Artibeus left the graveyard and arrowed upward. She passed through the Heaviside layer, trailing clouds.

Matthew John's Bat Rider phone rang. It was his parents.

'Hi, Mum. Hi, Dad. Tell Mr. Seeds he was right about Anoura. She gave me a horn.' He held the Wild Riders' horn up for his folks to see.

'Bless my soul!' said his mother. 'I thought Anoura was just a legend. I hope you didn't have to do anything dangerous.'

'Not really, Mum. We battled a headless king, fought off specters, solved a runic puzzle, and freed Anoura's Wild Ride. Oh, and Bulmer got turned into a ghost, but he's all right now.'

His mother gasped.

'We're proud of you,' said his father.

'Thanks, Dad. We're picking an exhaust trail. It may be Big Bad Bat's black ship. I'll talk to you later,' he closed his phone and slipped it into his pocket.

'What course, captain?'

Matthew John stroked his chin. 'It looks as though Big Bad Bat is heading for the Strange Loop Nebula,' he said. 'Let's follow him there. Bulmer, hop into the wind tunnel. Engineering, this is the captain. I want everything you've got.'

The Artibeus leapt for the stars.

CHAPTER III

Big Bad Bat Learns to Fly

'**I** WISH MY MUM AND DAD were here,' said Hannah Brianna, playing with the hem of her yellow dress.

'I miss my parents, too,' said Matthew John.

'This is my first mission,' said Hannah Brianna, 'I've never been away from home before.'

'The best thing to do is to keep busy,' said Matthew John. 'Here, have half my chocolate spider.'

'Thanks. The red eyes are neat. Mmm! They taste good, too.'

'The eyes are made of sprinkles.'

'Mr. Seeds gave me this book,' said Hannah Brianna with her mouth full. 'Will you read it to me?' She handed him a brightly colored volume.

Matthew John took the book. It was called BOGO THE LIZARD. On the cover of was a picture of a lizard dancing upside down on a ceiling. The lizard was green.

'The lizard looks cool,' said Matthew John, biting into his half of the chocolate spider. 'Are you sure you don't want to read the book to yourself?'

'I don't know all the words,' said Hannah Brianna.

Matthew John finished eating and opened the book. He began reading: '*Once upon a time there was a lizard named Bogo who lived in a book. "I wish I could crawl out of my book and live in the real world," said Bogo.* Do you want to turn the page, Hannah Brianna?'

Hannah Brianna turned the page. She wanted to see what was going to happen.

On the next page a real lizard was dragging himself out of a picture of a lizard. The front half of the lizard was in the real world but the back half of the lizard was still part of the book. 'It must be a pop-up book,' said Matthew John.

'I don't think so,' said Hannah Brianna, and turned another page.

The lizard ran out of the book and jumped into Hannah Brianna's lap.

'He's so cute,' said Hannah Brianna, tickling the

top of the lizard's head. 'He has a white patch on his little nose. Hi, Bogo,' she said. 'I'm Hannah Brianna.'

'Hi, Hannah Brianna,' said the lizard Bogo. 'I'm a dancing lizard, and not just any old lizard. I'm a gecko, and I have sticky feet. Put me on the ceiling.'

'You won't fall?' said Hannah Brianna.

'I told you. I have sticky feet,' said Bogo. 'I'll be all right. You'll see. Just put me on the ceiling. I love to dance on ceilings.'

'Matthew John, can you give me a lift up?' said Hannah Brianna, holding the lizard carefully with one hand.

Mathew John placed the book, still open, on the table. 'Climb up on my shoulders,' he said, crouching down.

Hannah Brianna stood on Matthew John's shoulders, and then Matthew John straightened his back slowly, balancing himself while holding Hannah Brianna's ankles.

Hannah Brianna reached up and put Bogo on the ceiling. She let go.

'Thanks, Hannah Brianna,' said the lizard. 'I have lots of room to dance up here.' He was hanging upside down by four sticky feet. 'Want to see my Bogo Bogo dance?'

'Show-off,' said Hannah Brianna. She jumped down from Matthew John's shoulders.

Hanging upside down from the ceiling, the lizard Bogo began to dance his Bogo Bogo dance. First, he lifted one leg, and then he lifted another. He sang 'Bogo, Bogo!' as he danced. His dance grew wilder. Now he had only two sticky feet touching the ceiling. He danced even more wildly. Now he had only one sticky foot touching the ceiling. 'Bogo, Bogo!' he sang as he danced.

'You'll fall,' said Hannah Brianna. 'That's enough dancing.'

'You haven't seen anything yet,' said Bogo. 'Watch this!'

Bogo the lizard went crazy. He took all four of his sticky feet off the ceiling.

'Bogooooooooo!' he cried, and fell from the ceiling. He fell into Hannah Brianna's Masterful Amazing Illusion Box.

Hannah Brianna ran to the Masterful Amazing Illusion Box. 'Bogo?' she said anxiously. 'Bogo, are you all right?'

Hannah Brianna reached down inside the box and felt about, trying to find the lizard. Her fingers closed on something warm and twitchy. 'I've got him,' she said, with a sigh of relief. Her fingers had found Bogo's tail.

She withdrew her hand from the dark cabinet and squeaked with surprise. 'Eek! I've got Bogo's tail,' she said, 'but where's Bogo?'

Bogo's tail squirmed in her hand, flicking this way and that. It felt funny. She burst into tears. 'I've killed him. I've killed Bogo.'

Matthew John switched on his flashlight and shone a powerful beam of light into the Masterful Amazing Illusion Box. The box was empty.

'I don't think you have killed Bogo,' said Matthew John. 'Lizards shed their tails when frightened. Wherever Bogo has gone, I expect he is okay.'

'No sign of Bogo,' he went on, 'but I do see some writing on the wall of the cabinet. The writing says "Masterful Amazing Illusion Box. Number One fun! Warning: Do not use Masterful Amazing Illusion Box in Strange Loop Nebula." I wonder why it says that.'

Matthew John tapped a key on his Bat Rider phone. 'Mr. Seeds? Are you there?'

'I'm here, Matthew John,' said Mr. Seeds's voice, 'and I have all of your parents here with me, eager for news. How is your voyage on the starship Artibeus going? Have you caught up with the Big Bad Bat yet?'

'We're hot on his trail. We've just landed on a planet in the Strange Loop Nebula, and Hannah Brianna's lizard has disappeared. Can you tell us how to get her lizard back?'

'Look about you carefully,' said Mr. Seeds, 'and tell me what you see.'

Matthew John turned on his heel, studying the strange landscape. 'It's all lizards,' he said, frowning. 'The floor is made of lizard-shaped tiles, there are lizard wall hangings, and the stairs have carpets decorated with lizards. Why is that?'

'In the Strange Loop Nebula,' said Mr. Seeds, '*what you see is what you seek.* If you wish to rescue Hannah Brianna's lizard, then you must go where the lizard went.'

'The lizard fell into the Masterful Amazing Illusion Box,' said Matthew John.

'Then you and Hannah Brianna had better follow the lizard into that Box,' said Mr. Seeds. 'Your parents and I wish you the best of luck.' The phone went dead.

Hannah Brianna wrapped the twitching lizard's tail in her handkerchief and stuffed it in her pocket. 'I must rescue him,' said Hannah Brianna, and she jumped into the Masterful Amazing Illusion Box.

'Hannah Brianna?' said Matthew John.

There was no answer.

'Bother,' thought Matthew John. 'This is all my fault. I'll have to go after her.'

A puff of cold air ruffled the pages of the open book about Bogo the Lizard.

Matthew John put a hand on the book to stop the pages being turned by the wind, and spotted a new picture on a fresh page, a picture of a bat dressed in a bright uniform. The bat had huge dark wings.

He pulled at his ear lobe. 'What is Big Bad Bat doing in Hannah Brianna's book about Bogo the lizard?' he wondered, and then recalled Mr. Seeds's words: *In the Strange Loop Nebula, what you see is what you seek.*

Matthew John closed the book and placed the volume carefully in his pocket. 'I must save Hannah Brianna,' he decided. He leaped into the Masterful Amazing Illusion Box, wondering where Big Bad Bat was, and what Big Bad Bat was up to.

Big Bad Bat was having a bad day. He was bouncing down a flight of stairs on his pogo stick.

The jewels on his pogo stick did not sparkle well in the half-light. Big Bad Bat had lost his followers. There was nobody to tell him what a really great bat he was. To make matters worse, he was still smarting from the defeat he had suffered not long ago on the planet Yumi, at the hands of that boy Matthew John. It was hard to imagine that he, Big Bad Bat, the most important bat in the whole universe, had been fooled by a mere boy like Matthew John, but he knew that he had been, all the same. Matthew John had reminded him of one of his earliest and most feverish memories, a memory of a day long ago when his toy tiger had peered in at him through his bedroom window, and he, Big Bad Bat, had been so frightened by this memory that he had ordered his black starship to take off at once and to leave the planet Yumi in a hurry, and in the rush of departure he had left behind four members of his crew and three valuable tree harvesting machines. It was all Matthew John's fault. One day he, Big Bad Bat, would get even with Matthew John. One day he would capture Matthew John and make him his slave.

A girl in a yellow dress came running up the stairs. 'Have you seen my lizard?' she asked. 'His name is Bogo.'

'No, I haven't seen your lizard!' snapped Big Bad Bat, bouncing on down the steps. 'You're the first person I've met for hours (bounce) I'm tired (bounce) and I'm fed up (bounce).'

'See you later,' said the girl cheerfully, and ran past Big Bad Bat and on up the stairs to continue her search.

Big Bad Bat bounced on down the stairs, wondering if he would ever reach the bottom stair. This crazy staircase seemed to go on forever.

For a second time the little girl in the yellow dress came running up the stairs. 'Have you seen my...? Oh, it's you again. I thought I passed you already. What's your name?'

'My name is Big (bounce) Bad (bounce) Bat (bounce),' said Big Bad Bat, 'and I am the most important bat (bounce) in the world (bounce) and no, I haven't seen your lizard (bounce) as I told you the first time (bounce).'

'I'm Hannah Brianna,' said the girl. 'Want to see my lizard's tail?' She unfolded a handkerchief and held up something revolting and wriggling.

Big Bad Bat turned his face away. 'Yuck!' he said. 'Keep that thing (bounce) away from me (bounce). I hate things that wiggle (bounce).'

'I want to give Bogo his tail back,' said Hannah Brianna, 'but I can't find him.' She wrapped the tail in her handkerchief once more and ran on up the stairs.

Big Bad Bat wiped the sweat off his forehead, and went bouncing on down the infuriating stairs. He muttered and grumbled to himself. He found it very hard work pogo-sticking down stairs. It made his feet ache.

For a third time the little girl in the yellow dress came running up the stairs. 'Have you seen…' she began, and then she stopped in her tracks. 'We've done this before,' she said, and stopped. She was puzzled.

Big Bad Bat, too, was puzzled. He stopped hopping down the steps. He paused on one step and remained there, seated on his pogo stick, with his wings half open to help him keep his balance.

He stared at the girl.

'We shouldn't keep meeting like this,' said Big Bad Bat. 'I'm the most important bat in the entire universe and you're just a girl.'

'The stairs go round in a circle,' said Hannah Brianna brightly. 'How shall we escape?' She pressed her thumbs to her forehead to help her think. 'I know,' she said, and smiled broadly. 'We'll leave the stairs and fly away together. You are a bat, aren't you?'

'I'm the most…' began Big Bad Bat.

The girl reached out, grabbed his left wing, and shook it. 'This is a wing, right?'

'Ooaaaah!" said Big Bad Bat, teetering dangerously. 'What are you doing? Let me go! I'll lose my balance.'

'Scaredy bat!' said Hannah Brianna, and let go of his wing.

Big Bad Bat lost his balance. He fell off his pogo stick. He landed on top of Hannah Brianna.

His pogo stick fell with a clatter and lay upon the stair, a thing of glittering metal and sparkling gemstones.

'Poof!' said Hannah Brianna, wriggling out from underneath Big Bad Bat. 'You're one big fat bat, that's what you are.'

'How dare you say such a thing?' roared Big Bad Bat. 'I exercise every day.'

'You don't even know how to fly.'

'I did once,' said Big Bad Bat. 'Long ago, I flew.'

Hannah Brianna clambered up onto Big Bad Bat's back and seated herself on his neck behind his ears. 'Don't worry, Big Bad Bat. I'll show you how to fly again. We'll fly together, you and I. I'm a bat rider.'

'You are?' Big Bad Bat was surprised that anybody as young as Hannah Brianna could be a bat rider. 'Ah… how long have you been a bat rider?' he asked, scratching his chin with his wing claw.

'Ages and ages, ever since the day before yesterday,' said Hannah Brianna.

Big Bad Bat spread his wings and shuffled awkwardly to the edge of the stair. He looked down. He did not like what he saw. 'We're awfully high up.'

Far below, Big Bad Bat saw water that tumbled from a great height only to be channeled back along canals to fall again. Floor tiles in the shape of lizards came to life for a few moments and then crawled back into floor. He saw upside down trees and stairs, and a girl waving, and a boy with a horn. He felt dizzy.

'I've changed my mind,' said Big Bad Bat, backing away. 'I don't want to fly after all.'

As he stepped back from the edge, he tripped over his pogo stick, scrabbled helplessly, remembered too late that his feet were attached to his wings, and shot out into nothingness. 'Help!' he cried. 'I'm falling!'

'We are both falling,' said Hannah Brianna, and grasped Big Bad Bat's neck tightly with her skinny arms. 'Keep your wings stiff. Try to catch the wind. You can do it, Big Bad Bat!'

Big Bad Bat was terrified. "L-like this?' he stammered. He made his wings as stiff as he could, and, to his surprise, something quite wonderful happened. He began to float through the air like a kite. 'Am I… flying?' he asked in a small voice, hardly daring to believe that it was true.

'Of course you are,' said Hannah Brianna happily. 'I can't wait to tell Matthew John. Here he comes!'

Matthew John leaped from the Masterful Amazing Illusion Box onto the tiled floor of a huge chamber. He saw large bat come flying towards him, and heard a familiar voice say 'You're coming in too low and too fast.'

Matthew John knew that voice. He cupped his mouth with his hands. 'Hannah Brianna?' he shouted. 'Is that you up there?'

'I'm riding this big bad bat,' Hannah Brianna shouted back. 'He hasn't flown for ages. He's excited. I can't get him to slow down.'

Matthew John saw the bat hurtling towards him. The bat was dressed in a blue frock coat with gold epaulettes. Matthew John knew of only one bat that wore clothes like that: Big Bad Bat.

Matthew John flung himself face down as Big Bad Bat swooshed past, and then stood up again.

Big Bad Bat circled around clumsily and then came rushing back to attack him again.

'I know who you are, Big Bad Bat,' Matthew John shouted. 'I have something important to say to you! I want to say I'm sorry.'

'Too late, Matthew John,' said Big Bad Bat, and dived down yet again, his claws bared.

Matthew John took cover in an art gallery. He dived straight through a twisted picture and into a street inside the picture. He ran down that street as fast had he could, but the faster he ran, the longer the street became. 'In the Strange Loop Nebula, what you see is what you seek' he reminded himself.

Matthew John heard the whistle of wind in Big Bad Bat's wings and glanced over his shoulder. Big Bad Bat had followed him inside the picture and was almost on top of him.

Matthew John jumped feet first down a manhole and ran along a tunnel under the street. What was he to do? His mind raced. Hannah Brianna was riding Big Bad Bat, but she did not seem to be able to control him. It was up to him, Matthew John, to find a way to control Big Bad Bat.

Matthew John ran out of the end of the tunnel and onto a rooftop. He saw Big Bad Bat flying by just below him, with Hannah Brianna seated on his neck. This is my chance, Matthew John decided, and flung himself off the roof. He sailed through the air.

Matthew John grabbed Big Bad Bat by his left ear and shouted:

'Hang on, Hannah Brianna!'

'Ow!' said Big Bad Bat. 'Let go of my ear. I'm the most important… Woo!' Big Bad Bat was thrown off balance and flipped over in the air. He began frantically flapping his wings to try to right himself. 'Help!' he cried. 'I've forgotten how to fly!'

With his free hand, Matthew John grabbed Big Bad Bat's other ear.

'How dare you grab my ears?' said Big Bad Bat. 'Don't you know who I am? I'm the most… Aieee!'

The hard tiled surface of the street came rushing up to meet them.

Matthew John let go of one of Big Bad Bat's ears and took hold of one of the lapels of Big Bad Bat's uniform coat instead.

Big Bad Bat somersaulted head over tail. He began to fall horizontally down the street. House after house flashed by on either side. 'This Strange Loop Nebula is even stranger than I thought,' said Matthew John to himself. 'We are falling *sideways*.'

Matthew John let go of Big Bad Bat's other ear and grasped the other lapel of Big Bad Bat's uniform coat. Now he had Big Bad Bat by both lapels, but still Big Bad Bat was hurtling through the air, and still he was out of control.

Matthew John and Big Bad Bat were face-to-face, eyeball-to-eyeball.

'I'm sorry I frightened you, Big Bad Bat,' said Matthew John quietly. 'I should never have reminded you of that tiger who looked in your bedroom window. I apologize, and I hope you will find it in your heart to forgive me.'

Big Bad Bat collided with a passing bird.

'Look where you are going!' squawked the bird, and gave Big Bad Bat a shove.

Big Bad Bat entered a spinning vortex of air. He went whirling around and around. 'You humiliated me in front of my crew, Matthew John!' he said. 'You'll be sorry.'

'I *said* I was sorry,' whispered Matthew John. '*Sorry, sorry, sorry, sorry.* How many times do I have to say I'm sorry?'

'Don't forget who you are apologizing to,' said Big Bad Bat. You are apologizing to *me*, the biggest, baddest bat the world has ever seen.'

'I taught the big bad bat how to fly,' said Hannah Brianna proudly, hanging on for dear life.

'I've been told that in this nebula, *what you see is what you seek*,' said Matthew John. 'Try thinking about where you want to go, Big Bad Bat.'

'I don't know what you mean,' said Big Bad Bat, and flew in through the airlock of his black ship. He hit the deck heavily, bounced and staggered to his feet. Hannah Brianna and Matthew John dropped down to the deck.

'Welcome back, great leader,' said Big Bad Bat's followers, bouncing about on their pogo sticks excitedly. 'We thought we had lost you.'

'Take Matthew John and Hannah Brianna away and lock them up,' said Big Bad Bat. 'I shall make them my slaves. I shall think up degrading jobs for them to do. Fetch me a pogo stick.'

Matthew John and Hannah Brianna were dragged away by the guards. They were imprisoned in the black ship's brig.

Bruised and sore, they looked questioningly at one another.

'Have the guards gone?' asked Hannah Brianna.

'I think so,' said Matthew John, peering out between the black bars of the cell at a wall beyond. 'I saw one of the guards hang his keys on a hook. Maybe I can reach the key ring...' He put his hand and arm between the bars and stretched as far as he could. 'No, I can't. The key ring is out of my reach.'

'If the lizard Bogo were here, he could crawl through the bars, run up the wall and get that key ring for us,' said Hannah Brianna.

'I suppose he could, if he were here,' said Matthew John, smiling.

Hannah Brianna stared down at the floor. '*What you seek is what you see,*' she said. 'Maybe Bogo *is* here.'

The floor of their prison was tiled. The tiles were white and green, and shaped like lizards. The white lizard tiles fitted neatly into the green lizard tiles. All of the lizards on the tiles looked exactly like Bogo.

Hannah Brianna knelt down on the floor. She stroked the white patch on the nose of one of the green lizard floor tiles. 'Bogo, Bogo!' she said softly.

The lizard put its head out of the tile. 'Hannah Brianna?' said the lizard. 'I'll dance if you'll help me out of this tile. Hold onto my front legs and pull.'

'Like this?'

Hannah Brianna pulled Bogo out of the tile.

'Thanks, Hannah Brianna,' said Bogo, and began to stretch his limbs, getting ready to dance.

Bogo moved one foot off in a half circle without touching the ground, and then rotated his hips. 'Bogo, Bogo!' he said to himself, and did a quick running side step. 'Bogo, Bogo!' he said. He danced across the cell floor. 'Am I good or what?' he asked excitedly, his little feet pattering on the tiles.

'You're the best dancing lizard I've ever seen,' said Hannah Brianna, 'but you need your tail for balance. Here, I saved it for you.' She pulled from her handkerchief the lizard's missing tail.'

Bogo's eyes lit up. 'My tail!' he exclaimed. 'I thought I should never see it again. Thank you, Hannah Brianna. Lift me up so I can kiss you on the nose.'

Hannah Brianna did what she was told.

The lizard kissed her on the nose.

'Now stick my tail back on please,' said Bogo.

'How?' asked Hannah Brianna.

'Just put the tail where it belongs,' said Bogo.

Hannah Brianna placed the twitching tail near the back of the lizard and the tail became one with the lizard again. 'Now that you have your tail back,' she said, 'would you mind dancing out between the bars of our prison and then dancing back with that key ring that's hanging from that hook on the wall? We need to make our escape.'

'No problem,' said Bogo. He ran up the wall on his sticky feet, and returned carrying the key ring in his mouth.

'Thwath a peethoake,' he said, by which he meant that fetching the keys had been a piece of cake.

Matthew John grinned. 'Thank you, Bogo,' he said, and took the key ring from the lizard's mouth.

'You're the best, Bogo,' said Hannah Brianna.

Bogo did a quick hop, skip and a jump.

Matthew John tried the keys. The second key turned the lock. There was a click and the door swung open. He stepped into the ship's corridor and glanced to left and right. 'All clear,' he said. 'Follow me!'

He ran onto the black ship's bridge, with Hannah Brianna at his heels. Bogo scurried along the ceiling.

On the bridge they found Big Bad Bat bouncing up and down. 'We have to get out of here!' he was saying. 'The Artibeus has come to look for us. (bounce) You call yourself a first officer? (bounce) Head for outer space!' (bounce)

'We cannot take off, sir,' the first officer replied. 'The hull of our ship is swarming with lizards.'

Big Bad Bat stopped bouncing. 'Lizards?' he said, puzzled.

The first officer sighed. 'A lizard is a small reptile…' he said.

'I know what a lizard *is*, you idiot,' said Big Bad Bat. 'What I want to know is: what are these particular lizards up to?'

'They are saying "Bogo-Bogo-Bogo." That is what they are up to.' The officer lowered his voice and brought his mouth close to Big Bad Bat's ear. 'I think Bogo must be the Lord of the Lizards, sir.'

'I want this Bogo person *now*,' said Big Bad Bat.

Bogo dropped from the ceiling and landed on Big Bad Bat's head.

'Aaaaa!' cried Big Bad Bat, flapping his wings to try to keep his balance. 'There's something on my head!'

Big Bad Bat shook his head violently from side to side. 'Whatever it is, it has sticky feet. I hate sticky feet! Get this creature off me, somebody! Save me!'

'I'll save you,' said Matthew John.

'Matthew John! What are you doing here?'

Big Bad Bat spun around. 'I locked you in the brig, Matthew John. You're my prisoner!'

'Oh, no, I'm not,' said Matthew John. 'I've broken out of your brig, and so has Hannah Brianna, and guess who helped us escape.'

'Who?'

'Bogo the lizard,' said Matthew John.

Big Bat Bat's eyes narrowed. 'The Lord of the Lizards? You know this Bogo person? Quick! Where is he? I have to talk to him.'

'He's on top of your head,' said Matthew John.

Big Bad Bat's eyes grew large and round. 'Bogo is on top of my head? The Lord of the Lizards is…?' He gulped. 'Ah, excuse me. Er. Lord Lizard, is that you up there? May I have a word with you, please?'

'Only if I dance on your head first,' said Bogo.

'Ah. Um. Yes, of course, anything you say, Great Lizard. By all means dance on my head!' said Big Bad Bat.

Bogo bent his knees and began to dance. As he danced he swayed from side to side, rotating his hips and making his little arms into the shape of an L while he pounded Big Bad Bat's skull with his feet.

'Enough!' cried Big Bad Bat. 'Stop dancing! I can't stand your feet drumming on my skull. I need your help!'

Bogo stopped dancing. 'How may I help you, Big Bad Bat?' he asked.

'The hull of my ship is crawling with lizards,' said Big Bad Bat, 'and the lizards are crawling all over my ship's sensors. My ship is blind. Help me!'

'Say please,' said Bogo.

'Please,' said Big Bad Bat, gnawing at his knuckles. 'Please, Lord of the Lizards. Do something.'

Matthew John waved his arms in a circle and pointed to his chest with his thumb.

Bogo nodded to let Matthew John know that he understood what Matthew John was trying to tell him. 'I shall tell my lizards to free your ship, Big Bad Bat, on one condition,' he said.

'What is your condition, great Lord of the Lizards?' said Big Bad Bat, gripping the handles of his pogo stick tightly.

'You must hand over command of this vessel to Matthew John,' said Bogo.

'That's outrageous!' shouted Big Bad Bat, and began to bounce up and down furiously on his pogo stick. 'Unspeakable! (bounce) You can't tell me (bounce) what to do (bounce) on my own ship (bounce).'

Bogo responded by doing the Hokey-Pokey.

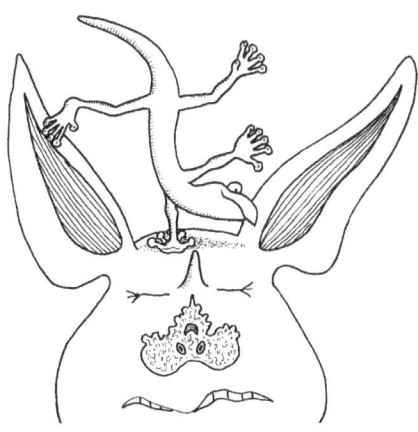

'Stop!' cried Big Bad Bat, and jumped off his pogo stick. 'No more Hokey Pokey on my head!'

'Do you give in, Big Bad Bat?' asked Hannah Brianna.

'Do you agree to our condition?' asked Matthew John.

'Yes, I give in,' said Big Bad Bat, 'and yes, I agree to your condition.' He grabbed his pogo stick with both feet and snapped the stick in two. Rubies scattered on the deck, winking red in the light of the ship's instruments. 'Yes, I agree to your condition. My ship is yours.' He flung away the two halves of his splintered pogo stick. 'Call off your lizard!'

'Come here, Bogo!' said Hannah Brianna.

Bogo sprang to the ceiling, ran along the ceiling tiles and jumped into Hannah Brianna's arms.

Hannah Brianna stroked Bogo's back with her finger and gave him a kiss. 'My, aren't you a clever lizard?' she said. She bent closer and whispered 'How do we get rid of all those other lizards, the ones that are swarming over the black ship's hull?'

'Don't worry,' Bogo whispered back. 'I'll tell the other lizards to go back into the tiles they came from. They are all copies of me, you see. I can tell them what to do.'

'I bet they look just like you,' said Hannah Brianna. 'I bet they all have a white nose patch.'

'Yes, they do.'

Matthew John flipped open his Bat Rider phone and spoke to the first officer in his own starship, the

Artibeus. 'I have taken command of the black starship. Power up the Artibeus and follow us out of the nebula.' He turned to the black ship's navigator. 'Lay in a course for the planet Yumi.'

The two starships, flying one behind the other, flew out of the nebula, trailing stardust.

Mr. Seeds's face appeared on the screen. 'You survived the Strange Loop Nebula?' he said. 'We were worried about you.'

The parents of Hannah Brianna and Matthew John could be seen in the background having tea with Mr. Seeds in his garden. They smiled and waved.

'The book you gave Hannah Brianna was really useful,' said Matthew John.

'Good,' said Mr. Seeds. 'I hoped that the book might come in handy. You had better tell that lizard Bogo to crawl back into his pages now, before the effects of the nebula wear off.'

'Do you hear that, Bogo?' said Hannah Brianna, sadly. 'You have to go back inside your book.'

'Do I have time for one last dance?' asked Bogo.

Hannah Brianna looked questioningly at Mr. Seeds.

Mr. Seeds nodded.

'Go for it, Bogo!' said Hannah Brianna.

Bogo jumped up in front of the screen and danced one last Hokey Pokey.

Matthew John and Hannah Brianna clapped and sang the Hokey Pokey song as he danced.

'*You put your right claw in, you put your right claw out, you put your right claw in, and you shake it all about. You do the Hokey Pokey and you turn yourself around. That's what it's all about!'*

When the lizard had finished his dancing, Matthew John took the BOGO THE LIZARD book from his pocket and handed it to Hannah Brianna.

Hannah Brianna opened the book.

Bogo leapt into the book and crawled back into a picture of himself.

'*And Bogo lived happily ever after,*' read Matthew John. 'Turn the page, Hannah Brianna.'

Hannah Brianna turned the last page.

On that final page of the book there was a picture of the lizard standing on one foot and grinning at them from ear to ear. The lizard was waving goodbye.

'He looks happy,' said Hannah Brianna, and closed the book gently so as not to hurt her friend. She raised her eyes and gazed at Matthew John. 'I'm glad we're going home,' she said.

Matthew John smiled at her. 'So am I,' he said.

CHAPTER IV

Mr. Seeds and the Locusts

'WHEN I WAS YOUNG,' said Mr. Seeds, 'I liked to explore strange places. One day I ventured into a forest of towering, straight trees beyond Big Cat Canyon. The air smelled of geraniums. The trees were old and many were hollow, for the living part of a tree lies just beneath the bark, and when a tree grows old, the dead wood at its heart is often nibbled away by insects. The trees were decorated with pale and spotted orchids. Among the trees were flies that flashed and flickered with blue light. It was lovely but scary, so I sang a little song to keep my spirits up:

> *I wish I had a bat*
> *To fly me through the sky*
> *I'd give my bat a hat*
> *And say 'It's time to fly!'*

'I wish I could!' said a strange voice.

'Who are you?' I asked, peering about. I saw nobody.

'I'm Hoh-Kay,' came the reply.

'If you're okay, why call for help?'

'Hoh-Kay is my name. I'm stuck inside this tree. Hurry up and let me out!'

'What tree would that be?' I asked, warily. I was surrounded by trees.

'Over here,' said the voice. 'Buck up! I'm starving.'

By the light of the flashing flies I searched and found at last a hole in a hollow tree and saw an eye looking at me. 'Why can't you climb out?' I asked, keeping my distance.

'Because I'm too big,' said the creature inside the tree. 'I can't get my wings through the hole. It's too small.'

'You have wings?' I said, my hopes rising. 'What kind of creature are you?'

'No idea,' said the voice from the tree. 'I've just been born. I'm probably a flying squirrel or something, but I'll never find out if I don't get out, so get a move on and rescue me. All sorts of yucky spiders and creep-crawly things are tickling me in here. Are you going to help me?'

'I'm thinking of the best way to help you,' I said, which was not quite true, for I had yet to think of *any* way to help the whatever-it-was out of the tree it was trapped in.

After a while, I had an idea. Perhaps the tree itself

might help.

'Er, tree,' I said. 'Can you hear me?'

The tree answered at once. 'Yes, I can hear you.'

'There's some kind of an animal stuck inside you.'

'It's a bat,' said the tree.

'Wow!' I said. 'Is there any way I can let the bat out? I want to be a bat rider.'

'Crawl inside me,' said the tree. 'Through the hole in my bark.'

'If I do that, we'll both be stuck inside you, won't we?' I scratched the back of my head.

'Not really,' said the tree. 'I'm a hollow tree as you can see. My trunk is open to the sky. If you climb inside me and then sit on the bat's back, you and the bat should be able to fly up to the top of my trunk, and escape that way.'

'I'll try,' I said eagerly, even though I had never ridden a bat before. 'Keep back, Hoh-Kay!' I said to the bat. 'I'm coming in to join you.'

I put my feet inside the tree and wriggled and kicked. My foot hit something soft.

'Ow!' said Hoh-Kay. 'That's my head.'

'Sorry, Hoh-Kay,' I said. 'It's a bit of a tight squeeze.' I held my arms straight above my head and wriggled some more. 'I think I'm stuck,' I said, breaking out in a sweat.

I felt a claw grab my ankle and pull. I slid inside the tree in a shower of bits of bark.

'Thanks, Hoh-Kay.'

It was hard to see inside the tree, for only a little daylight shone in here and there from holes in the bark. Craning my neck, I spotted what looked like a tiny pinprick of light about a mile above our heads. If that was our way out, then I should have to fly Hoh-Kay up there. Could a bat fly so high in so narrow a place? I didn't know.

'We'll learn to fly together,' I said.

'I'll sit on the back of your neck and hold onto your fur, and then you'll flap your wings, and we'll both go up into the air.'

'What for?' asked Hoh-Kay, brushing a spider from his face.

'There's another, better world waiting for us at the top of the tree. Trust me. There are clouds, flowers and delicious Yumi fruit to eat. You'll love it. We just have to get up there.' I felt about in the dark and seated myself astride Hoh-Kay's neck. 'Go on, Hoh-Kay!' I said excitedly. 'Beat your wings! I'll steer!'

'Hoh-Kay beat his wings and we flew up, up, up, spinning around and around in the narrow interior of the tree, until we shot out of the top of the tree and into the fresh night air where we found ourselves flying among the flashing flies, and breathing in the heady perfume of the orchids.

'And that was how I became a bat rider,' said Mr. Seeds. 'I had no idea that my greatest enemy, Instar, was being born on that same night on the border of that same forest.'

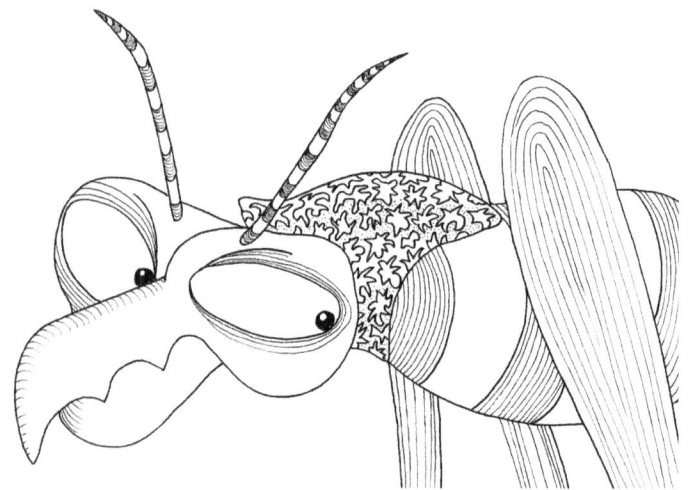

Instar crawled out of the froth and sat for a few moments in the sunshine. Strange creatures with bulbous eyes and huge back legs surrounded him.

'Feeling itchy?' said one of the creatures.

'Itchy?' said Instar. He shook his head.

'You will be,' said the creature. 'Soon you'll begin to itch all over.'

'I think I'll do some exploring first,' said Instar. 'Want to come?'

'No,' said the creature. 'It is just grass.'

'Suit yourself,' said Instar, and hopped away on his own. He came to a footprint.

'What kind of animal would make a footprint this big?' he wondered. He bumped his nose on a round green pea. 'This round green thing smells yummy,' he thought. He sniffed the pea. The pea made his mouth water. It had the aroma of fresh green things warmed by the sun. Mmm! He spent an hour eating the entire pea. It was delicious. When he had finished, his skin began to itch, so he wriggled out of it.

Ah! That felt better! He looked down at his empty skin lying on the ground. It looked like a deflated collapsed insect. He nudged the empty skin with his nose. 'That was me,' he thought. 'That was Instar the First. But now I am the new me. Now I have a fresh skin so I need a fresh name. I'll call myself Instar the Second.' He spied a whole pod full of ripe beans that smelled rich, smoky and tender. It took him a week to eat them. As soon as he had finished the last of the beans, he began to scratch himself. 'How many more times shall I shed my skin?' he wondered.

Instar shed his skin four more times until he became, in the end, Instar the Sixth. Admiring his own reflection in a puddle, Instar the Sixth thought how important and handsome he looked. He was far bigger than any of the other locusts. It was time for him to eat the world.

'I am the Instar the Sixth, Lord of the Locusts,' he told his fellow locusts. 'Follow me and I shall give you more food than you have ever dreamed of!'

With these words Lord Instar took off, and millions of his brothers and sisters took off with him. They flew together to a meadow near Mount Boom and ate every bush, flower and blade of grass.

'I was Lord of the Locusts years ago,' he recalled, 'and a boy riding a bat challenged me to a duel. He said he was trying to protect the Yumi trees. We fought on the lip of a volcano and I cast that boy down.'

The memory of his ancient triumph gave Lord Instar new confidence.

'Nobody will dare challenge me this time,' he went on, 'for I am the biggest and scariest locust in the universe. Attack the Yumi trees, my brothers and sisters!'

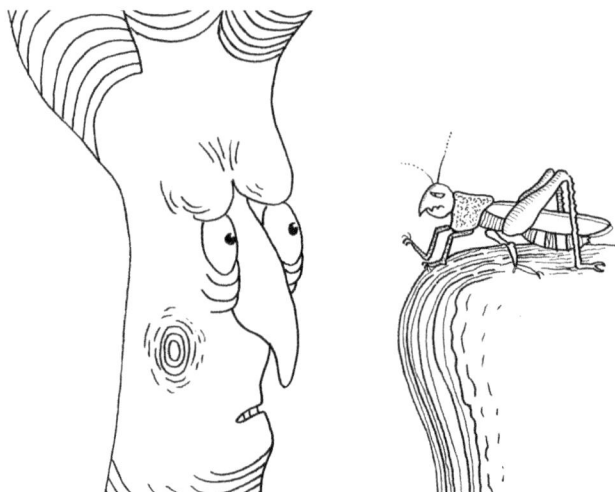

When the Yumi trees saw the cloud of locusts approaching, they knew that their ancient enemy had been reborn.

'Don't worry,' said Boris, who was a stouthearted tree. 'Have no fear, my fellow trees. Stand fast! Matthew John will save us from these wicked locusts.'

'Matthew John is our hero,' Boris went on. 'He has saved us before. He will save us again. Trust me. Matthew John won't let us down.'

Matthew John's friend Emily Charlotte was on duty in the Bat Cave Watchtower. She saw the cloud of locusts coming and grabbed her bat rider phone.

'Matthew John?' she said anxiously. 'Matthew John, can you hear me?'

There was no answer.

Matthew John was not answering his phone because he was in his bedroom playing with his toy bat Pudding, so when his phone began to tremble in his pocket, he did not notice.

'No more adventures,' he was saying to Pudding. 'They've made me Air Chief Marshal of the Bat Riders of Yumi.'

Pudding made no reply, for he was a stuffed toy.

Matthew John waggled Pudding's wings. 'It was fun while it lasted, Pudding,' he went on. 'I flew high above the treetops. I felt the wind in my face. I saw the Strange Loop Nebula.'

Matthew John flew his toy bat over to the round window of his room, where his breath fogged the glass.

He rubbed a hole in the condensation with his fingers. It was a bright sunny day. He could see his parents. Mum was snipping bits off a rose bush with a pair of shears, while Dad was making holes in the ground with the handle of a rake. Matthew John pressed his nose to the pane and watched his father drop a single Yumi tree seed into each of five holes and cover the holes carefully with soil.

'I wish something exciting would happen, Pudding,' he said.

The sky darkened.

A cloud passed in front of the sun. It did not look like any cloud Matthew John had seen before. Matthew John abandoned Pudding and craned his neck to have a better look. The cloud was rushing towards him.

'The cloud knows where it is going,' he said to himself, and felt a shiver of fear.

A creature slammed into the windowpane.

It gnashed its jaws and stared hungrily at Matthew John through the glass. The creature was yellow-green with black spots and stripes that decorated six legs, four wings, a segmented body, and two bulges on the top half of its face. It looked fierce, as though it was trying to eat its way through the glass. Matthew John wondered what kind of creature it was.

Another similar animal hit the window, and then another. Matthew John ran out of his room and into the living room. He flung open the front door of his home. A thousand yellow-green and black insects flew into the house, their rainbow wings whirring. Some of the insects grabbed at his clothes, while others crawled over his bare skin.

'Yuck!' he said, brushing the creatures off with his hands. 'Mum? Dad? Are you all right?'

His parents staggered through the doorway, their arms around one another's shoulders. They were both covered from head to foot in insects.

Dad spat one of the insects from his mouth. 'Help me close the door,' he said.

Matthew John and his father pushed the door shut. The insects were piled a foot deep outside. More were arriving every second.

Matthew's mother pulled an insect from her son's hair. 'Are you all right, Matthew John?' she asked.

'I'm fine,' said Matthew John, brushing some of the flying beasts from his mother's arms and legs with his hands.

'What are these things? Where did they come from? What shall we do?'

'When caught by surprise, close your eyes,' said his father.

'Oh, Dad, you are so silly! Mum?'

'They are locusts,' said his mother. 'They have come to eat the plants in our garden. Locusts are greedy.'

'What about the Yumi trees?' asked Matthew John quickly. 'Will these locusts eat the leaves of Yumi trees?'

His mother nodded. 'I'm afraid they will,' she said.

'I'm Air Chief Marshal of the Bat Riders,' said Matthew John. 'I have to save the trees. But how?'

'You had better ask Mr. Seeds,' said his mother. 'He dealt with a swarm of locusts when he was a bat rider. He'll know what to do.' She held the locust she had pulled from her son's hair at arm's length.

Matthew John's phone hooted. It was the bat rider emergency signal!

'Excuse me,' said Matthew John, dragging the phone from his pocket.

'Is that you, Matthew John?' said the voice of Emily Charlotte.

'Yes,' said Matthew John.

'I've been trying to reach you,' said Emily Charlotte. 'The Bat Cave is swarming with yellow-green insects with black stripes. They are eating all the moss, and I can't seem to reach Mr. Seeds.'

'Make sure the baby bats are safe, Emily-Charlotte,' said Matthew John. 'I'll go and talk to Mr. Seeds in person.' He closed his phone, put two fingers in his mouth and whistled for his bat Wimpy.

'You are not thinking of flying your bat out into that swarm of locusts?' said his mother.

'I have to, Mum,' said Matthew John. 'Mr. Seeds is not answering his phone, and the trees may be in danger.'

Matthew John ran out of the living room into the atrium, leapt onto the back of his bat Wimpy and flung open the skylight. 'Let's go, Wimpy!' he cried.

Wimpy took off. He and Matthew John flew out of the house and into the cloud of locusts.

'We should not have let him go,' said Matthew John's mother.

'He's our best hope,' said Matthew John's father.

Matthew John clung grimly to Wimpy's fur. It was hard to see where they were going because the air was thick with flying locusts. The din of their wings was unceasing. 'Higher, Wimpy!' he cried, and felt the flight muscles of his bat ripple under him as she fought to gain height.

Wimpy was scared. Her every wing stroke scattered the locusts like snowflakes, yet she could feel her skin crawling with more of them, and her wing

strokes were slowing. Soon she would be too heavy to fly. 'We're not going to make it,' she said.

'Yes we are!' repeated Matthew John, and squeezed his bat's flanks with his knees. 'Look! The cloud is thinning.'

He could see the edge of the cloud of locusts.

A moment later they burst into clear cold air, high above the swarm.

Matthew John pulled locust after locust from Wimpy's fur, and flung the brittle half-frozen insects away until his bat could fly more easily.

'Here is the Bat Cave Watchtower,' said Matthew John.

Matthew John and Wimpy were glad to see their friends Emily Charlotte, Joshua Ryan, and Hannah Brianna waiting for them. 'How bad is it?' asked Matthew John as he leapt from Wimpy's back to the wooden deck of the tower.

'We're being eaten alive,' said Emily Charlotte's bat Vesper.

Emily Charlotte patted her bat's neck. 'Cheer up, Vesper. Matthew John's here. Everything will be all right, now.'

'Has the swarm reached the Enchanted Grove?' asked Matthew John.

'Locusts fly at a speed of nine feet per second,' said Joshua Ryan. 'They'll be there in five minutes.'

'We must not lose a moment,' said Matthew John. 'I have a mission for you, Emily Charlotte and Joshua Ryan. I want you to fly straight to the Artibeus. I am appointing you Starship Captain, Emily Charlotte. You are to serve as Science Officer, Joshua Ryan.'

'And me?' piped up Hannah Brianna, jumping up and down with excitement. 'Can I do something too?'

Matthew John crouched down and grasped the little girl firmly by her shoulders. 'Yours is the most important job of all, Hannah Brianna.'

'I am appointing you Lieutenant of Lizards,' Matthew John went on. Do you have your BOGO THE LIZARD book with you?'

'Yes,' said Hannah Brianna.

'Is your bat Bulmer close by?'

'He's hanging upside down from the bottom of the tower platform.'

'Good. Tell him he is to navigate the starship for you. He is to take the Artibeus back to the Strange Loop Nebula. The moment you arrive there, Hannah Brianna, I want you to coax that pet lizard of yours out of his book and tell him we need an army of lizards just like him. Okay?'

'Okay,' said Hannah Brianna, her eyes shining.

Matthew John let go of Hannah Brianna and stood up. He looked at Emily Charlotte. 'I want you to come back here with a starship full of lizards,' he said.

'Yes, Air Marshal,' said Emily Charlotte.

'Yes, Air Marshal,' said Joshua Ryan.

'Yes, Air Marshal,' said Hannah Brianna.

'Are you coming with us?' asked Hannah-Brianna, hopefully.

Matthew John shook his head. 'No,' he said, 'I have to talk to Mr. Seeds.' He vaulted onto Wimpy's back and took off once more. They swooped through the chilly air.

'I wish we could see Mr. Seeds's house,' he said to Wimpy. 'Eep! Eep!' she cried, and listened to the echoes of her cries bouncing back from the ground below. 'There it is,' she said proudly. 'I can see his D-shaped door.'

'Well done, Wimpy!' said Matthew John.

Wimpy closed her eyes, folded her wings and plummeted back into the cloud of locusts. She slammed into scores and scores of the horrible creatures, sending them flying in all directions. At the very last moment she spread her wings wide, hovered, and landed.

Matthew John slid from Wimpy's back.

'Mr. Seeds!' he sang out.

He opened the door.

'Mr. Seeds? Are you there?'

'In here, Matthew John,' said Mr. Seeds.

Matthew John ran into the living room. 'Mr. Seeds! There's a swarm of …' He stopped in his tracks, too astonished to finish his sentence.

Mr. Seeds had a visitor.

Big Bad Bat was sprawled across Mr. Seeds's settee, his gaudy uniform glittering with medals, and his gold epaulettes winking in the lamplight.

'Welcome, Matthew John,' said Mr. Seeds. 'I'm glad you have come. A locust ate my phone and I could not reach you.'

'The swarm of which you speak is led by Lord Instar, an old enemy of mine. That is why I have asked Big Bad Bat to join us. He and I fought Instar many years ago.'

'You flew together?' said Matthew John, looking first at Mr. Seeds and then at the Big Bad Bat and then back at Mr. Seeds again.

He had never thought of the two as a team. 'You were his rider and he was your bat?'

Big Bad Bat stared at Mr. Seeds, and his mouth fell open. Apparently this was news to him, too.

'The Lord of the Locusts,' Mr. Seeds went on, 'is not just my enemy but the enemy of the Yumi trees in general and of all that we hold dear.'

'Our enemy Instar is reborn once every generation,' Mr. Seeds continued, 'usually after a heavy rain, along with millions of his brothers and sisters. Last time that he crawled out of his skin, I was as young as you are, and I held the rank of Air Chief Marshal of the Bat Riders, the very same rank that you now hold, Matthew John, so it was up to me to face Instar and to find a way to defeat his swarm.'

'What did you do?' asked Matthew John.

'I challenged Lord Instar to aerial combat,' Mr. Seeds replied. 'The Lord of the Locusts rode on the back of his praying mantis Armageddon, while I rode on the back of my bat Hoh-Kay. It was a fierce fight. Just when victory seemed within my grasp, the Lord of the Locusts touched his mantis's left eye with the tip of his antenna, and that wicked mantis Armageddon grabbed my bat Hoh-Kay by the head, and, locked together, we fell into Mount Boom!

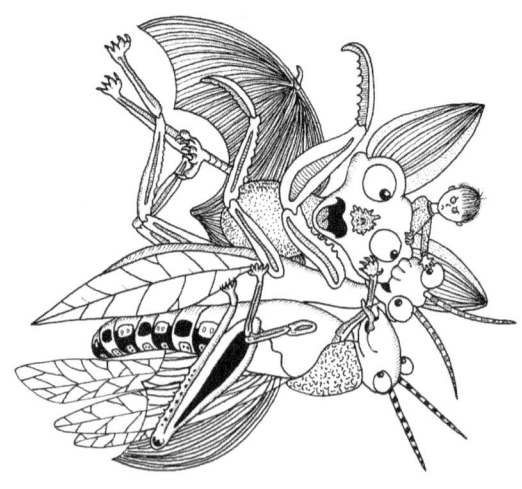

'We crashed into a rock ledge. The praying mantis Armageddon had the wind knocked out of her. She let go of Hoh-Kay and slid off the ledge. The Lord of the Locusts dived after her. His followers dived after him. All the locusts disappeared into the volcano.

'Hoh-Kay and I were left on our own. We had won our duel. We had saved the Yumi trees, but something was dreadfully wrong with Hoh-Kay.

"I'm BIG," Hoh-Kay kept saying, frothing at the mouth, "I'm BAD, and I'm a BAT."

"Can you help me?" I asked Hoh-Kay gently. "My legs don't seem to work any more."

"You address me as Big Bad Bat," said Hoh-Kay.

My heart sank. My faithful bat was nuts.

"Big Bad Bats don't fly," he added, as if that explained everything.

'I put my arms round my bat's neck and hugged him. "I don't blame you for not wanting to fly again, Big Bad Bat, not after what you have just been through," I said, "but can you crawl at all? You and I have to leave this ledge soon or we shall be baked to a crisp by this volcano."

"Yes, Big Bad Bats can crawl," he replied, and dragged me into a cave in the crater wall. There he hoisted me on his back and carried me home through the lava tubes. As he dragged me along he kept saying over and over: "I'm BIG, I'm BAD and I'm a BAT." He was very determined, and I was proud of him.'

Mr. Seeds turned to Big Bad Bat, who had been listening to the story with rapt attention. Matthew John could see by the expression on the bat's face that he remembered little or nothing of this.

'You saved my life that day, Big Bad Bat,' said Mr. Seeds. 'I thanked you then and I thank you again now, from the bottom of my heart.'

Big Bad Bat looked down at his uniform coat. 'I was bitten by a praying mantis and went bananas? My real name is Hoh-Kay?'

'Yes, that is your real name,' said Mr. Seeds. 'Your fellow bats used to tease you about it, I'm afraid. They used to say 'Are you okay, Hoh-Kay?' and then laugh.'

'Perhaps I'd better stick with my new name,' said Big Bad Bat.

'It is lucky that Hannah Brianna and Matthew John have taught me to fly again,' Big Bad Bat went on. 'I shall have to face this Lord of the Locusts. Who shall ride on my back this time?'

'I'll ride on your back, Big Bad Bat,' said Matthew John. 'If that's all right with you, Wimpy?'

Wimpy nodded eagerly. She had had enough adventures to last her a lifetime.

Matthew John flung open the skylight. Whirring locusts filled the room.

Matthew John climbed onto Big Bad Bat's back. 'Let's find this Lord Instar,' he said, and they took off.

Lord Instar was not far off, crouching in the bushes, eyeing a praying mantis.

The mantis was clinging to a twig and keeping very still. She was disguised as a green leaf.

'You lucky mantis!' said the Lord of the Locusts. 'You have been chosen to bear me into battle. Your reward shall be an entire platoon of my finest soldiers.'

'Do they have crunchy heads?' whispered the mantis.

'Yes,' said the Lord of the Locusts. 'Yes, very crunchy. All I ask is that you allow me to ride on your back. How's that for a bargain?'

'I am yours to command,' hissed the mantis. 'My name is Annihilation, but you may call me Annie.'

The Lord of the Locusts sprang onto the mantis's back.

'Fly us to victory, Annie!' he said, and went forth, mounted on Annihilation, into the fumes of Boom, and his swarm was with him, and his coming was a wonder.

Electricity crackled in the air. Pyroclastic bombs exploded.

A fierce wind rocked the Yumi trees.

Terror stalked the land.

'I am Instar the Sixth!' cried the Lord of the Locusts. 'I claim this forest as my own! Does anyone dare challenge me?'

'I do,' said a small voice.

'Who speaks? Show yourself!'

'I'm Matthew John,' said the boy, 'and I am riding the bat who defeated you the last time you attacked this forest. So stop and think, Lord Instar. Why destroy these Yumi trees on which the lives of my people depend? We bat riders can find plenty of food for you and your host. Let us make peace.'

The Lord of the Locusts leaned forward and whispered to his mantis.

'I hear and obey, Lord Instar,' hissed the mantis. 'It shall be as you ssssay.'

The Lord of the Locusts raised his voice. 'There can be no peace between us, boy. What do sea monsters eat?' He raced towards Matthew John.

'Fish and ships,' answered Matthew John, ducking down between Big Bad Bat's ears. He and Big Bad Bat swooped down under the mantis's belly. 'What's in the middle of Kanji?' he shouted back.

'The letter 'n' is in the middle of Kanji,' the Lord of the Locusts replied, taking his mantis around in a steep climbing turn. 'You'll have to ask better riddles than that to defeat *me*, Matthew John.'

Matthew John and the Lord of the Locusts wove around one another in the air, striving for mastery of the world.

Without warning the Lord of the Locusts struck Matthew John with one of his powerful back legs.

Matthew John was knocked sideways. He hauled back hard on Big Bad Bat's epaulettes and cried 'Two can play at that game, Instar!'

Matthew John and Big Bad Bat bumped into the mantis's tail.

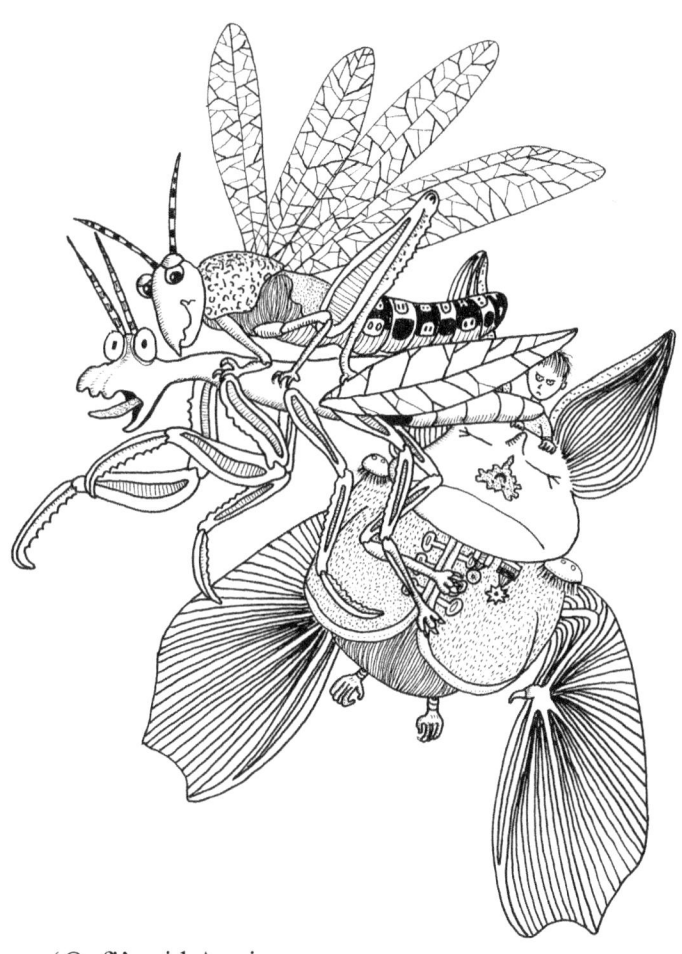

'Oof!' said Annie.

'Why did the banana go to the doctor?' roared the Lord of the Locusts.

Matthew John tried to think of an answer. The reply had to have something to do with banana peel. He dodged a flaming volcanic bomb.

'Well?' said the Lord of the Locusts. 'Can you answer my question?'

The answer came to Matthew John in a burst of inspiration. 'Because the banana wasn't peeling well,' he said, and zoomed past Annie.

He thumbed his nose at Lord Instar.

The Lord of the Locusts dived after him.

More puns shot back and forth.

Matthew John asked a question the Lord of the Locusts could not answer. He followed it quickly with another just as difficult. 'I'm winning,' he thought. 'I have to ask only one more unanswered question and I shall win.'

A shifty look came into the eyes of the Lord of the Locusts.

Matthew John saw Instar bow his head and tickle the mantis's eye with his antenna. It was the same signal that Lord of the Locusts had used in his fight with Mr. Seeds long years ago.

Quickly Matthew John swung Big Bad Bat into an emergency Hammerhead Stall Turn.

Annie's front limbs shot out to grab Big Bad Bat, but missed.

Matthew John rolled Big Bad Bat over in the air and raced back to surprise the Lord of the Locusts from above and behind. 'What goes up but never goes down? Quick! Answer me, Instar!'

'Nothing,' the Lord of the Locusts snapped back, upset that his ruse had failed. 'All that goes up must come down,' he added, hastily.

Hot rocks flew up into the air and fell down again.

'Wrong answer,' said Matthew John. 'The answer is 'age.' Your age goes up but it never goes down. That's the third riddle of mine that has stumped you. Our duel is over. Do you concede defeat?'

'Never!' cried the Lord of the Locusts.

'Sssssss,' said Annie, and seized Big Bad Bat's uniform jacket with her spiked forelegs. 'I'm a praying mantisssss,' she hissed. 'I never let go.'

Locked together, the mantis and the bat, the locust and the boy, fell through the air into the yawning mouth of Mount Boom.

The volcano rumbled. Matthew John caught a glimpse of bubbling lava. He felt a wave of searing heat. They were falling to their death. He reached for the buttons of Big Bad Bat's uniform coat and undid the first button, and then the second. He was running out of time.

'Take off your coat,' he shouted in Big Bad Bat's ear, struggling with the third and last button. 'Help me.'

Big Bad Bat wriggled out of his coat.

Matthew John and Big Bad Bat were free!

Annie the praying mantis, her forelimbs caught up in Big Bad Bat's uniform jacket, vanished into the volcanic fumes, and the Lord of the Locusts vanished with her.

Matthew John felt dizzy. The volcanic fumes were going to his head. He tried to steer Big Bad Bat up into clearer air, but Big Bad Bat was weakening.

'We are in trouble,' he thought. 'Where is the Artibeus? What's keeping them so long?'

Matthew John's life hung in the balance. Only his starship could save him now.

Captain Emily Charlotte paced up and down the bridge of the starship Artibeus, trying not to step on the lizards. The lizards on the deck were not very quick at getting out of her way because of the jet packs strapped on their backs, while the lizards on the deck head kept firing their jet packs to stop themselves from falling, so the air was full of smoke, and Emily Charlotte could hardly see the screen.

'Is that the planet Yumi?' she asked, fanning the smoke with her hands.

'I'm not sure,' said Bulmer, his voice echoing in the wind tunnel as he beat his wings furiously. 'Does it have trees a mile high? Does it have a huge moon?'

'Yes,' said the captain.

'That's the place,' said Bulmer, panting. 'Any sign of Matthew John?'

'Not yet. Take us down.'

'Aye, aye, captain,' said Joshua Ryan. 'We're picking up signs of life from the region of Mount Boom. It's Matthew John and Big Bad Bat. They are falling into a crater.'

The Artibeus roared over the forest, filling the hills with the thunder of her passage.

'Launch the lizards!' ordered the captain.

'Geckos away!' said Hannah Brianna.

One hundred lizards fired their jetpacks and roared out of the starship. They tore through the air towards Matthew John and Big Bad Bat.

The lizards grabbed Matthew John and Big Bad Bat with their claws, and bore them safely back to the ship.

'Land the ship in the Enchanted Grove,' said Emily Charlotte.

The starship settled on the mossy forest floor on the grove, amid the greatest of the trees of Yumi. Millions of lizards scuttled out of the ship. They scattered through the forest, running up the trunks of the trees and out onto the branches to defend the trees against the locusts.

It was lizard against locust.

The battle went on all night and all the next day. Every time a locust landed and began to chew on a Yumi tree leaf, a lizard gobbled up that locust. Soon every locust in the swarm had been eaten. The lizards returned to the ship, looking fat and happy and licking their lips.

They had tasted victory.

'Well done, Captain Emily Charlotte!' said Matthew John. 'You have won the battle and saved the trees. Ferry the lizards back to the Strange Loop Nebula, and then ask Hannah Brianna to make sure her personal lizard Bogo crawls back into his book. I'll meet you later at Mr. Seeds's house.'

The catering for the Victory Party was placed in the capable hands of Annabelle Sue of the Jelly Belly Restaurant, assisted by her father Chef Wandor. The guests ate Mantis Cream Pie, Chocolate Instar Cake and Locust Surprise Pudding. The entertainment for the party was provided by Armando the Lion Tamer and his Lion Oomba. Also invited were Baagh the tiger and her daughter Kiti, the schoolteacher Miss Pretty Flower, and the well-known vegetarian leopard Hyou from the island of Kanji, who brought a dozen glowing snails along to liven up the evening. Big Bad Bat came to the party, too, and offered to be Mr. Seeds's bat again, just like old times, and tears came to Mr. Seeds's eyes as he said yes.

Then Mr. Seeds wheeled his chair in among his guests, banged a spoon on a wineglass for silence, and said: 'Air Chief Marshal Matthew John will now present medals to three deserving people who helped save our planet.'

'This medal is for you, Emily Charlotte,' said Matthew John, 'to remind you of your successful first mission as captain.'

'Thanks,' said Emily Charlotte. 'I had a great time with the lizards.'

Matthew John pinned the medal on her dress.

'This medal is for you, Joshua Ryan,' said Matthew John, 'for having the idea of fitting out the lizards with jet packs.'

'It was the logical thing to do,' said Joshua Ryan.

'And this third medal is for you, Bulmer,' Matthew John went on, 'for navigating the starship so well.'

'Thanks,' said Bulmer, happily. 'All that flying in the ship's wind thingy has strengthened my muscles, so I'm strong enough to carry you again, Matthew John, if you want.'

'I'd like nothing better,' said Matthew John.

It was one of those wonderful nights when all the stars were strewn across the sky like diamonds. Matthew John and Bulmer did not know where they were going, but that did not seem to matter. When two close friends are reunited after being apart, just being together is enough.

CHAPTER V

Matthew John Blows his Horn

MATTHEW JOHN's mother entered Matthew John's bedroom and picked up his stuffed toy bat. She held the stuffed toy at a distance while holding her nose with her other hand. 'You need a bath, Pudding,' she said.

Pudding tried to say that he did not want to have a bath but he had not yet learned to speak. He could not even say how uncomfortable it was for him to be carried along swinging by one ear.

Matthew John's mother opened a round glass door in the side of her washing machine and thrust Pudding inside. She closed the washing machine door and pressed a button.

Pudding's world gave a lurch and began to move to and fro in a sickening fashion. Pudding was turned over and over. Water was sprayed in his face. The water tasted of soap.

'Yuck!' thought Pudding. 'I'm inside a washing machine. I'm being tossed about. It's hard to think. If only the machine would stop.'

The machine began to spin. It spun Pudding around. It spun him faster and faster.

Pudding became scared. 'Help!' he shouted. It was his first word.

Matthew John's mother did not hear Pudding's first word because the washing machine was too noisy. When the spin cycle ended, she took Pudding out of the machine and hung him up to dry outside in the garden. 'You smell better now, Pudding,' she said.

Pudding was too shaken to reply. He made up his mind to escape as soon as he could. He did not want to be put into a washing machine again. As soon as Matthew John's mother went back inside the house, Pudding tried to move his wings.

He felt his wings move!

He tried to move his feet. He felt his feet move!

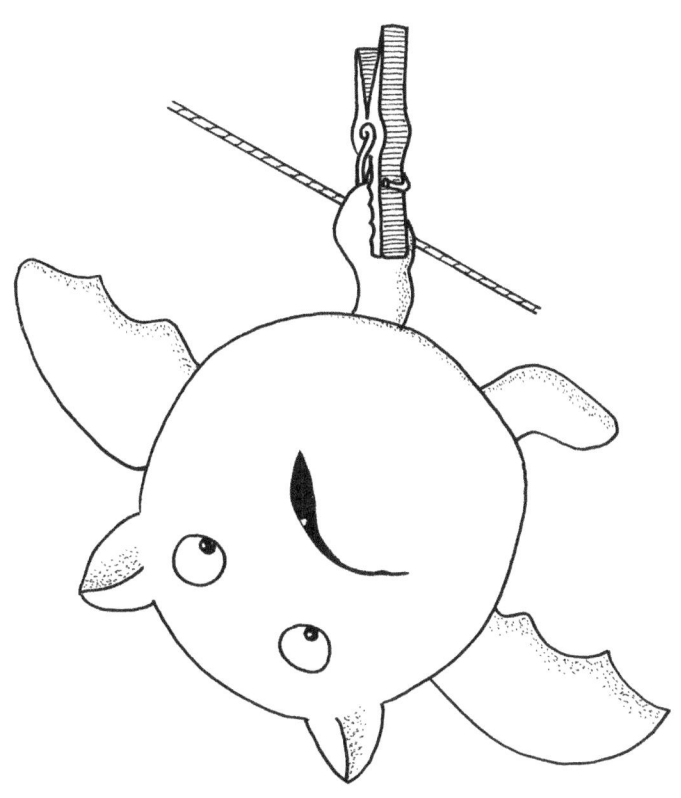

His feet kicked themselves free of the clothesline!

It was amazing. His body was working! It had never worked before. He had come to life. At least, he assumed this was life.

Pudding went sailing away through the air. There was a big flash. Lightning hit a tree. Fire broke out. Pudding smelled smoke. He heard something roaring and crackling.

'I wonder if I'll ever see Matthew John again,' he thought.

'What's that?' asked Matthew John's mother.

'It's my phone ringing,' said Matthew John. 'Hello? Annabelle Sue, is that you? What? Mount Boom has disappeared? You must be joking!' Matthew John opened the sliding door and ran out into the garden. 'You're right. I can't see Mount Boom at all, and the whole sky has turned orange. I'll meet you at the White Cave.'

'You may wish to take this with you,' said Matthew John's father, taking down the horn of Anoura from its hook on the wall above the fireplace and handing the instrument to Matthew John.

'Thanks, Dad,' said Matthew John. He tucked the horn into his belt and rode his bat Bulmer up into the orange sky.

A warm updraft bore them aloft.

Bulmer, his wings spread wide, enjoyed the feeling of floating in the rising air. 'I'm a balloon,' he said.

'I wonder why we can't see Mount Boom even from up here,' said Matthew John, brushing flakes of pale white stuff from his bat's neck.

'Maybe the mountain has floated away like a balloon,' said Bulmer dreamily.

'I think the mountain is still there but is hidden by smoke,' said Matthew John. 'Do you smell burning?'

Bulmer wrinkled his nose. He nodded. 'Somebody's having a bonfire,' he said.

'Look!' said Matthew John, pointing to a glow in the distance. 'That is too big for a bonfire. The forest itself is burning. There is Annabelle Sue at the mouth of the White Cave. Can you land beside her?'

'Me? Land beside her?' said Bulmer. 'No problem. I'm a flying ace, remember?''

Bulmer performed a spectacular inverted roll and somersaulted through the air. He bumped his head on the roof of the cave and crashed into a pile of salt.

'Whob did I tell yoob? No ploblam.'

Matthew John slid down the pile of salt. 'Have you a plan for putting out the forest fire, Annabelle Sue?'

'No.'

'Send for the firefighters!' said Matthew John.

A hundred bat riders jumped off the backs of their bats and began to walk purposefully towards the blazing forest. As they fanned out in front of the wall of flame, they beat at the smoldering vegetation with pogo sticks, while their anxious bats hovered overhead in the billowing smoke, fanning themselves with their wings. The smoke thickened. It became hard to breathe.

Matthew John and Annabelle Sue grabbed pogo sticks for themselves and ran to help, but the fire would not go out. Flames raced along the ground, leaping from bush to bush. An exploding thorn bush sent up a fountain of sparks and thorns. The wind veered suddenly, sending the blaze leaping across the valley.

A crackling wall of pink, crimson and scarlet flames bore down on the firefighters, and their bats dived to save them.

Matthew John and Annabelle Sue stumbled back into the White Cave, their bats at their heels, and threw down their pogo sticks.

'The fire is winning,' said Annabelle Sue.

They felt a wave of scorching heat roll over them. More choking smoke rolled into the cave.

'If only the wind would change,' said Annabelle Sue, and coughed. She could taste the smoke.

'Maybe if we asked the wind nicely…' said Bulmer.

'I met somebody once who could control the weather,' Matthew John said, and reached for his horn.

'That's the horn Anoura lent you?' asked Annabelle Sue.

'She said I was to sound it if I needed help.'

'What are you waiting for, then?' asked Annabelle Sue. 'The forest is on fire. We *need* help.'

121

Far away in the Strange Loop Nebula, at the famous bat-riding school of Leafnose, Anoura woke in her dormitory with a start. Had she heard the cry of a distant horn? Or had she been dreaming? She threw off her bedcovers and ran to the window, her bare feet complaining of the cold stone. Her twenty Wild Riders were hurrying to fetch their bats. Something was up! She ran to the chair beside her bed and pulled on her bat riding gear. She fastened her waistband hurriedly.

She ran down the corridor and paused under the arch leading to the school kitchen. The cook and her husband lay asleep by the hearth. Anoura tiptoed in and took a jug of juice from the table without waking them.

She ran to the bat roost and scratched Bat between his ears. 'How are you doing, Bat?' she whispered. 'I brought you a treat.' Bat opened his big eyes wide.

'My favorite,' said Bat, slurping up the juice from the jug. The juice tasted of Yumi fruit.

Anoura climbed onto Bat's back.

'Let's go, Bat!' she cried.

Bat spread his wings and shot out of the loft.

Anoura felt cold air on her face. She was flying! She and her bat went soaring through swirling clouds.

Lightning spat and crackled around them.

'Warooo!' bellowed the horn again.

'Sizzling specters!' cried Anoura. 'Someone is in trouble! To me, my Wild Riders!'

Her twenty faithful followers rose from the wood in a whir of bats' wings, and then her brother Mimon flew up to join them, riding his bat Wallop.

'Matthew John is sounding my horn,' said Anoura.

'I told him to blow the horn if he needed our help,' she went on to say. Her bracelet flashed in the light of First Sun. 'Great Ia!' she shouted. 'Take us to boy with the horn!'

'Ia!' shouted her Wild Riders and her brother.

A brilliant white flash lit up the heavens.

Anoura and her riders were transported to the planet Yumi. They found themselves flying over a strange landscape of mile-high flaming trees, while above their heads a storm cloud rumbled.

'The Great Bat of Evening has brought us to the planet where the boy with the horn lives!' she shouted above the roar of the fire. 'Find him!'

'The sound of the horn is coming from that cave!' shouted King Mimon, pointing.

'Groaning goblins!' cried Anoura. 'Follow me, everyone!'

Anoura swooped down towards the cave.

Inside the cave the smoke from the forest fire was making it hard for Matthew John and his friends to see one another.

'Let's blow the horn one last time,' said Annabelle Sue. 'Matthew John has blown the horn, and so have I, and so has Emily Charlotte. Now it's your turn, Joshua Ryan.'

Joshua Ryan raised the horn to his lips.

'Warooo!' said the horn.

A huge bat slammed into a white pillar of salt, and a man in royal robes slid down from his bat's back. 'At times like this I wish my sister hadn't reattached my head to my body,' he said.

'King Mimon!' said Annabelle Sue. 'You look better with your head on.'

'Your majesty,' said Matthew John. 'Thank you for coming to help us in our hour of need.'

'Me?' said King Mimon. 'I'm just here because

my sister Anoura gave me a bat to ride called Wallop, and whenever Anoura and her Wild Ride take off on some mission or other, Wallop wants to join them. Whatever has she bumped into this time?'

'Your bat has bumped into a column of salt,' said Joshua Ryan.

'It's all right, Wallop!' said Bulmer, hobbling over to help the capsized bat. 'Don't worry about crashing into things. I do it all the time.'

'You do?' said Wallop. 'I thought it only happened to me.'

Bulmer grinned. 'Give me your claw. My name's Bulmer.'

'Creaking caskets!' said a voice from the smoke. 'I can feel the Boy with the Bat close by. Matthew John?'

'Anoura?' said Matthew John. 'Is that you?'

'Chattering skeletons! Of course it's me. You blew my horn, didn't you? Who were you expecting?'

Anoura strode out of the smoke. Reflections of the flaming forest danced in her eyes.

'We have a forest fire to put out. Can you help us?' said Matthew John.

'Screaming banshees!' said Anoura. 'How do you expect me to help you fight a fire?'

'Your brother,' said Matthew John, 'is a weather scientist. Can he make it rain?'

'Last time I experimented with weather I lost my head,' said the king, fingering his neck nervously.

'All we have to do is seed that cloud,' said Matthew John, pointing to a storm cloud visible from the cave entrance through a gap in the smoke. 'We need to make that cloud rain.'

'Impossible!' said the king. 'To make that cloud rain we'd have to drop particles of fine salt into the top of the cloud. We'd need tons of salt.'

'This cave is full of salt,' said Matthew John.

The king looked about him. He picked up a pinch of the white powder and rubbed it between thumb and forefinger. 'This might be fine enough, but where are the hundreds of bat riders we would need to sprinkle the salt on top of the cloud?'

'I have twelve hundred bat riders at my command,' said Matthew John. 'But we must hurry. The fire is racing towards our houses, and our parents are in danger.'

The work of seeding the cloud began at once.

Matthew John rode Bulmer up through suffocating blue smoke, his backpack in one hand. A burst of crimson sparks exploded around them.

'Wow-ooo-raa-ah!'

'Uh. What's that?' said Bulmer, biting his lip.

'It's the wolves. They are trying to escape from the fire,' said Matthew John. 'Loopy!' he shouted. 'Is that you?'

The big male wolf skidded to a halt, his son Bonkers at his side. 'Matthew John?' he said, staring up at the boy riding his bat.

'Head for the White Cave, Loopy,' Matthew John said, pointing up the hill. 'Your family will be safe there.'

'Thanks,' said Loopy.

'Follow me,' said Loopy's wife Loo to her son Bonkers.

'I'm not going to hide in no stupid old cave,' said Bonkers. 'I'm going to bare my teeth and frighten the fire away.'

'You're going to do as you're told,' said his mother. 'You're not the alpha male, yet, Bonkers.'

'I will be,' said Bonkers.

127

Matthew John squeezed Bulmer's flanks with his knees. 'It's going to be a close call, Bulmer,' he said, and flipped open his phone. 'Akihito Akemi! I want Number One Squadron to help me seed the cloud over the Enchanted Grove.'

'I hear and obey, honorable master,' said the voice of Akihito Akemi.

'We have a fighting chance, Bulmer,' said Matthew John. 'Antonina Vladlena and her Number Eight squadron are seeding the north end of the cloud, while Hui Chen and his Number Ten squadron are doing the same at the south end. Take me up higher. You and I have work to do in the middle.'

Up they shot, the boy and his bat, higher than the highest tree, higher than the leaping flames, higher than the writhing smoke, up, up, up into the heart of the thundercloud.

'Woo!' said Bulmer. 'I feel like an express elevator.'

'We're riding an updraft inside the cloud,' said Matthew John. 'I haven't been this high since I went to the Moon. I'm feeling quite light-headed.'

'My voith is going all squeaky,' said Bulmer.

'Ith the altitude,' squeaked Matthew John. 'Ith affecting our voiceth.'

'Quack!' said Bulmer, trying out his new voice.

'Bulmer, thith ith a therious mission,' squeaked Matthew John. His voice sounded like an angry little mouse.

'Yeth, Matthew John,' said Bulmer. 'I muth keep a grip on myselth. I muth not quack up.'

Boy and bat shot out of the top of the cloud into starlight. Other bat riders joined them. The top of the cloud looked like a fluffy blanket spread out below them.

'Cast your thalt on the cloud, bat riderth!'

He dug into his backpack, grabbed a handful of the white powder from the cave and cast the grains onto the cloud. He watched the fine particles wink and glitter as the cloud swallowed them.

'I hope this works,' he thought, and reached for more.

Back and forth Matthew John and the other the bat riders flew, seeding the cloud. They went on seeding until there was no salt left in their backpacks, and then went down to the White Cave to fill up their backpacks with more.

Matthew John lost track of how many times he

made the journey high into the sky to sprinkle more salt on the cloud. Each fresh journey was scarier than the one before.

Suddenly something dark loomed large.

'Look out, Bulmer!' said Matthew John.

Bulmer bumped into another bat.

'Oops!' said Bulmer. 'Sorry.'

'You can't do that to me,' said the other bat. 'I'm BIG, and I'm BAD and I'm…'

The wings of the two bats became tangled together.

Riders and bats tumbled head over heels out of the bottom of the cloud and hit a burning tree. They slid down the tree's trunk, and landed in a heap at the bottom.

Big Bad Bat wrenched his wings free.

A very small, very fierce tigress jumped out of a burning bush and stood glaring at Big Bad Bat. She arched her back and twitched her tail. 'I AM DEATH WITH TEETH,' she said.

Kiti's mother, the huge tigress Baagh, leaped out of the smoke and landed beside her daughter.

'Baagh,' said Matthew John. 'It's good to see you and Kiti. The forest is burning. Mr. Seeds can't walk and Big Bad Bat has lost his nerve. Can you carry them both to Mr. Seeds's house?'

'Yes,' said Baagh.

'Thank you, Baagh,' said Matthew John. 'Up you go, then, Mr. Seeds! And you, too, Big Bad Bat!' He helped the pair up onto the tigress's back, and Baagh bounded away through the flaring forest with Mr. Seeds and Big Bad Bat on her back and Kiti running at her side.

'Can I eat the bat?' said Kiti.

The tigresses vanished into the smoke.

Matthew John's phone alarm rang. It was the emergency signal.

'Matthew John here.'

'The forest fire is nearing the mouth of the White Cave,' said Joshua Ryan, 'and we can't get out.'

'I'm coming,' said Matthew John, and he and Bulmer flew back to the White Cave. 'Can you fly through flames, Bulmer?'

'Easy-peasy,' said Bulmer, bravely. 'Who cares about a few silly old flames?'

Bulmer shot into the blazing cave mouth.

Matthew John smelt singed fur. Poor Bulmer!

As they landed inside the cave, a falling tree missed them by inches. A red hot boulder, dislodged by the dying tree, slammed into the cave entrance. The boulder was too hot to touch.

By the crimson light of the glowing boulder, the bat riders stared at one another.

'We're done for,' said Emily Charlotte's bat Vesper. 'We're trapped in a cave. We'll all going to be burned alive.'

'While there is life there is hope,' said Anoura. 'Great balls of fire! We are not defeated yet.'

Matthew John picked up a shattered branch and touched one end of the branch to the hot boulder. The branch burst into flames. 'Let's see where this cave leads,' he said.

Holding the flaming branch on high, he strode into the darkness. He was frightened of the dark.

Deep under the mountain the bat riders went, their bats hobbling after them, until they came to the end of a long tunnel and found the way barred by a rock wall.

'We've come to a dead end,' said Vesper, shaking her head, 'just as I thought we would. Now we'll all be choked to death by the smoke.'

Matthew John held the flaming branch up higher. Dark shadows advanced and retreated, hinting at ledges and crannies. 'I don't see a way out,' he said, frowning.

He stepped back to have a better look.

Something squeaked under his foot.

He looked down and saw a familiar face looking up at him.

The stuffed toy Pudding was lying on his back on the rough rock floor.

'Pudding?' Matthew John said, leaning down to pick up the stuffed animal. 'What are you doing here?'

He held up Pudding for his friends to see. 'I've found my toy bat Pudding,' he said. 'I can't imagine how he got here.'

'He must have fallen down from above,' said Joshua Ryan, 'which means that there may be a way for us to reach the open air.'

Matthew John stuffed Pudding into the front of his shirt. 'You may have saved our lives, Pudding,' he said.

'Wow!' thought Pudding. 'I'm a hero.' He was too shy and too modest to say this out loud.

Matthew John and his friends mounted their bats and flew up to the height of the cave to explore the rock ceiling.

'Sizzling serpents!' cried Anoura, and pointed to four lines of runes carved in the rock:

'What do the runes mean, Anoura?'

Anoura's lips moved as she formed the ancient words. 'WHEN ALL ELSE FAILS THIS TUNNEL TAKE, BUT DO NOT LET GREAT IA WAKE.'

'I'll go first,' said Matthew John, and he and Bulmer flew into the dark opening of the tunnel in the cave ceiling.

'My ears tell me there is something or someone moving about up ahead,' said Bulmer. His voice sounded loud in the confined space of the tunnel.

'Try to keep calm,' whispered Matthew John. 'Keep your voice down.'

'Too late,' said Bulmer. 'Whatever it is, it has found us.'

Something knocked the flaming tree branch from Matthew John's hand, and the flames went out.

'Uh-oh,' said Bulmer. 'The thingy has come to get us.'

Matthew John's mind raced. What kind of creature had they woken? Why had it struck at his torch? Was the creature afraid of the light?

'Who's there?' said Matthew John, trying to sound confident and brave.

He hated the dark. It gave him the willies. If only he could see. 'Who are you?' he asked.

'I am Ia,' said a voice.

'Ia, we are bat riders. We are trying to put out a forest fire. The mile-high Yumi trees are burning. May we pass through your passage to reach the sky? It is a matter of life and death.'

'Is Anoura with you?' asked Ia.

'I am here,' said Anoura.

'I brought you and your Wild Riders here, Anoura. I would hate you to fail in your mission.'

'Thank you, Great Bat of Evening,' said Anoura.

'If I open up this passage to the sky I shall not be able to send you home again,' Ia went on to say.

'I understand.'

'So be it,' said the voice of Ia. 'What I do now, I do for all bats everywhere. May your wings be strong and your hearing keen. May your children's children people the caves of a thousand worlds. I shall not see you again.'

The mountain shook. Rock shattered and split.

'The night sky!' said Emily Charlotte.

'The constellation of the Great Bat,' said Joshua Ryan.

'Shining stars!' said Anoura. 'The mighty Ia has sacrificed herself to open the mountain for us.'

'Follow me!' said Matthew John, and he and Bulmer flew up out of the shattered rocks and into the starry heavens.

Matthew John flipped open his phone and spoke to First Seed, the oldest and wisest of the mile-high Yumi trees. 'The flames are nearing your Enchanted Grove, First Seed,' he said. 'Ia has split the mountain and we bat riders have filled the cloud with salt, yet I see no sign of rain, and I fear for your life.'

'Do the best you can, Matthew John,' First Seed replied in her pleasant and resonant voice.

Matthew John and Bulmer flew out of the bottom of the cloud. A gust of wind send the forest fire leaping into the Enchanted Grove.

Matthew John gasped. The flames were everywhere. It was like an oven. His heart sank. He could see First Seed, the greatest of all trees, blazing from bottom to top. Her bark was ablaze. Her mile-high trunk was a pillar of fire. Tears coursed down Matthew John's cheeks. It was the worst moment of his life.

He had failed in his most important mission. First Seed had been the wisest and most gentle tree he had ever met. It had been First Seed who had taught him to see the good in Big Bad Bat, and inspired him to dare the Strange Loops Nebula and to bring Big Bad Bat home. Above all other Yumi trees, Matthew John had wanted to save First Seed from the fire, but now First Seed was burning, and it was all his fault. He would never again hear her voice or visit her beautiful garden in the sky.

'Rain, you stupid cloud!' he cried, tears streaming down his cheeks. He shook his fist at the sky 'Rain!'

'Barabambadoom,' replied the cloud.

Something wet hit Matthew John's head. It was a raindrop. He looked up.

'My nose is wet!' said Bulmer.

The rain grew stronger and soon became a deafening downpour, drumming the ground and sending up clouds of hissing steam. Lightning lit up the sky. Thunder shook the heavens. The rain turned into a torrent that swept through the forest. The trees stopped burning. The rain poured down the shaft made by Ia and into the White Cave, threatening to drown those trapped inside.

'Artibeus,' said Matthew John. 'I'm at the mouth of the White Cave. 'I need a dinosaur. Quickly.'

The starship Artibeus landed with a whump in the wet ash, the cargo bay door flew open and a dinosaur named Bronto charged out. Matthew John pointed at the boulder blocking the ruined entrance to the cave. Bronto slammed into the boulder headfirst and sent the big rock rolling away.

Out of the shattered cave poured the hundreds of trapped bat riders and their bats, borne along by a great flood of rainwater.

When they saw Matthew John standing there with Bulmer at his side and the rain pouring down on his head, they all began to clap and cheer.

From every side people soaked to the skin ran to pat Matthew John on the back and shake his hand.

'Matthew John! Matthew John!' they shouted. 'Three cheers for Matthew John!'

When the cheering died down, Matthew John held up a hand for silence.

'First Seed has died,' he said, brushing a tear from his cheek. 'Let us go to her tree garden.'

The bat riders and their bats flew to First Seed's tree garden, where they found the carefully pruned bushes singed and the roof of the arbor caved in.

'The rain came too late,' Matthew John said as he jumped down from Bulmer's back and ran splashing through the ash and mud along a branch. He came to the towering trunk of First Seed. He put his hand on her scorched and blackened bark. 'I'm sorry, First Seed,' he said quietly. 'I'm going to miss you. I should have acted sooner. I should have found some way to save your life.'

'Eerk!'

Matthew John looked about him, puzzled. What had made that strange sound?

The sound came again: 'Eerk! Awk!'

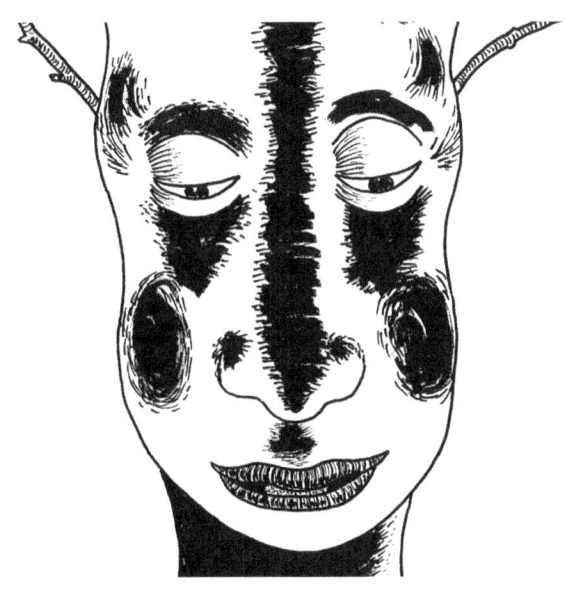

Matthew John looked up at the dark bark of the tree.

'What's that sound?' he asked.

Flakes of burnt wood and charcoal fell away to reveal two cheekbones, a hint of two bright eyes, and a pair of lips that parted slightly to blow out a cloud of black soot.

'First Seed?' Matthew John whispered, hardly daring to believe that the oldest tree in the world had survived the fire.

First Seed puffed up her cheeks. 'Thank you for saving our forest, Matthew John,' she said.

'But you are burned from top to bottom,' said Matthew John, 'and so are your brothers and sisters. You must all be dying.'

'We are not dying,' said First Seed. 'We Yumi trees *like* fire. We encourage fire. Fire is our friend. Our sap burns merrily in a forest fire, and the orchids in my garden need to be scorched by a forest fire before they can flower. Now that you have brought this fire to an end, I shall shed my old bark and replace it with fresh bark, and I shall take pleasure in watching my orchids bloom.'

Matthew John was amazed. 'I don't understand,' he said. 'How can you be unhurt, First Seed?'

'The fire did me little damage,' First Seed explained, 'because the living part of me is safe from fire, protected by my bark. That is true of many trees.'

'I see,' said Matthew John. He turned to the solemn crowd of bat riders and shouted so that all might hear the good news: 'First Seed lives!'

Cheers and whistles greeted this excellent news. Bat riders and bats jumped up and down with joy.

'First Seed,' said Matthew John, turning back to face the tree, 'I am very happy for you, and for all the other Yumi trees. Did your peacock survive?'

'I sheltered him from the fire inside my hollow interior,' said First Seed. 'Here he comes now.'

'Howrrrr!' said the peacock.

Matthew John tickled the peacock's head. 'I suppose the relationship between trees and fire will be one of those things I shall learn more about when I go away to school. My teacher Miss Pretty Flower says that I have to leave home soon in order to see the big picture.'

'Your teacher is wise,' said First Seed. 'Now that you have blown Anoura's horn, it is just possible that Anoura may invite you to go back with her to Leafnose school and to study there. Leafnose is an ancient academy with much to offer, in my opinion.'

In a whir of wings, Anoura landed her bat on one of First Seed's burned branches.

'How many of you blew my horn?' asked Anoura.

'Four of us,' said Matthew John, 'Emily Charlotte, Joshua Ryan, Annabelle Sue and me. Here's the horn back.'

He handed her the magical horn.

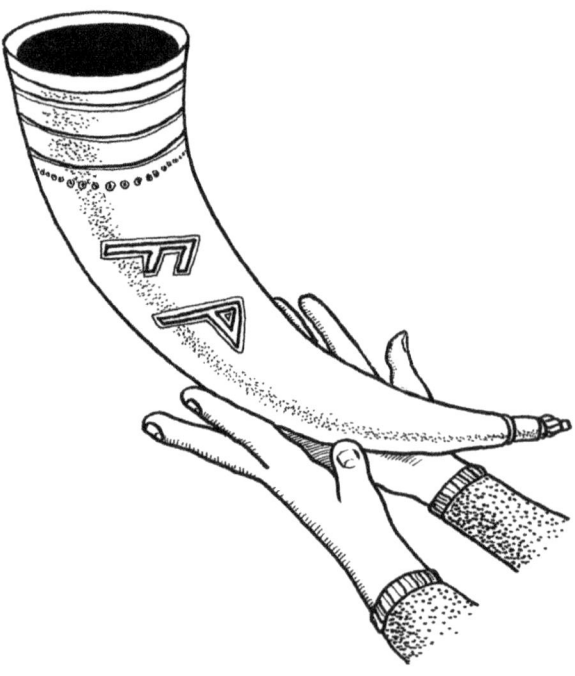

Anoura accepted the horn. She made up her mind. 'I invite the four of you and your bats to attend my Leafnose School for Bat Riders,' she said.

'We'll have to talk to our parents about that,' said Matthew John.

'If you are heading for home to talk to them,' said Mr. Seeds, who was rubbing Make-You-Better Butter on Bulmer's singed wings. 'I think I should like to go back to my house, too.'

'I'll fly you home, Mr. Seeds,' said Big Bad Bat, who had recovered his wits as well as his flying skills now that the forest fire had been put out.

Matthew John helped Mr. Seeds up onto the back of Big Bad Bat. 'Bulmer and I will fly back with you,' he said. 'It is on our way home.'

The first thing Matthew John did when he got home was to toss Pudding onto his bed.

The second thing he did was dump his salt-encrusted backpack on the floor. 'I'm home!' he shouted. 'Anoura's invited me to go to her school. It's called Leafnose.'

'Leafnose?' said Matthew John's mother. 'Isn't that the famous school for bat riders?'

'Yes,' said her son. 'Mr. Seeds went to Leafnose. He says they have a pteranodon.'

'Pteranodons are dangerous,' said his Mum, frowning.

'The more we brave, the closer we shave,' said his Dad.

'Miss Pretty Flower says I should go,' said Matthew John. 'She says the school has a high reputation, and will broaden my outlook.'

'Will any of your friends be going with you?'

'I hope so. They are talking to their folks now.'

Mum sighed. 'Well, I suppose you can go to Leafnose if you want to, Matthew John, but I wish you had chosen a school that was nearer home.'

'I'm afraid I'm to blame,' said her son. 'I was the first to blow Anoura's horn, you see.'

'You blew the horn that saved us all from the fire?'

'Yes.'

'Then we're proud of you,' said Mum.

'Don't forget to write home,' said Dad. 'I want to hear all about that pteranodon.'

'I have some clothes and things ready for you,' said Mum.

'I'd better hurry up and pack,' said Matthew John, shaking the last of the salt from his pack.

146

He crammed a bunch of clothes and toothbrushes and other things in. He bundled up the golden hourglass from the black ship in one of his old shirts, and stuffed that in, too, for good measure. You never know. An hourglass might come in handy one day.

He looked at Pudding lying on his bed and wondered if he should take Pudding.

It might not be safe to do so. There was that pteranodon. He did not want Pudding eaten.

'Goodbye, Pudding,' said Matthew John. 'Sorry you got all covered in soot.'

Pudding did not answer. He stared up at the ceiling, his eyes bright, his foolish little wings open and his large floppy bat ears spread on the pillow. He said nothing. He had had quite enough of life. Being alive was hard work. He hoped nobody was planning to put him back in the washing machine.

'We're going to have to fly the Wild Riders back to the Strange Loop Nebula,' said Matthew John to his mother.

'Why?' she asked from the next room.

'Ia, the Great Bat of Evening, gave her life to free us from the White Cave and to save the forest, so now it's up to us to see Anoura safely back to her home. Anoura will ride with us in the Artibeus,' he explained.

'Mmm,' said his mother in a voice which told him she was not really listening. Matthew John felt uncomfortable when she did not listen to what he had to say. Did she think it was all just a game he was playing?

He ran into the living room.

'I can't believe I'm going away,' he said out loud, staring about him at the familiar room and wondering if he would ever see it again.

'You are not going away,' said his father, 'until you take the first step.'

'Oh, Daddy! I have to learn how starship engines work and I have to study the flies that live in the fur of bats. Miss Pretty Flower says that small things are as important as big things.'

'Do you agree with her?'

Matthew John put his head to one side and looked at his father. 'Yes, I think so. I have to learn how everything fits together.'

'That's the first step,' said Daddy. 'The second step is to shake your father by the hand and say goodbye.'

They shook hands. 'Goodbye, Dad. Goodbye, Mum. What are you going to do with Pudding?'

'He's covered in soot from the fire. He's going straight back in the washing machine,' said Matthew John's mother.

There was a squeak from the bedroom.

'Poor old Pudding,' said Matthew John. 'Two washes in one day.'

His mother looked out of the window. 'I see your friends waiting for you at the Look Out Place.'

The Look Out Place was the little hill where Matthew John had first observed bat riders flying overhead on that long-ago day when he had decided that he wanted to become a bat rider himself.

So much had happened to him since.

The hilltop was badly burned. All the leaves were gone from the branches of the trees, the trunks had been blackened, and the rain-soaked ash on the ground felt damp and soggy under his feet.

'About time you showed up,' said Annabelle Sue.

Matthew John grinned at her. 'They have a pteranodon. Mr. Seeds told me. And a ship in a tree, and a ha-ha.'

'A ha-ha?' asked Emily Charlotte. 'What's a ha-ha?'

'I have no idea. Miss Pretty Flower says you can climb down into it.'

'I expect I'll fall into it,' said Bulmer.

'It's probably dangerous,' said Emily Charlotte's bat Vesper. 'I expect we'll all die.'

'I hope they have a science lab,' said Joshua Ryan. 'I've packed all my specimens.'

'So. Are we going or what?' said Annabelle Sue.

'We're going,' said Matthew John. 'I've left Hannah Brianna in charge of the squadrons. She has a brand new bat to fly called Wingy-Thingy.

They found Anoura and her Wild Riders waiting by the airlock, and entered the starship with them.

'Uh, I hope they have landing lessons at this school we're going to,' said Bulmer, looking at King Mimon's bat Wallop.

'I hope so too,' said Wallop, and she batted her eyelids at Bulmer. 'We could crash into things together.'

'All aboard?' said Matthew John, striding onto the bridge.

Captain Emily Charlotte nodded. 'Bronto is back on the Dinosaur Deck. We're all set to go.' She turned to the duty officer. 'Take us up,' she said.

From the window of their house, Matthew John's parents watched the starship take off. The sky was still stormy but the wind was dying down.

'I hope Matthew John will be all right,' said Matthew John's mother.

CHAPTER VI

Saying Goodbye to Pudding

'P UDDING HAD TO STAY behind,' says Pinky, 'even though he saved Matthew John's life.'

'Matthew John couldn't take Pudding with him to his new school in case he was eaten by the ptera-thingy,' says Suki.

'The pteranodon,' I say.

'Shall we ever see Matthew John again?' asks Pinky, frowning.

'I'm not sure,' I reply. 'He might come home for the holidays.'

'If he does, will he tell us about his new school?' asks Suki.

'I'm sure he will.'

'Pudding will like that,' says Pinky.

THE BAT RIDERS AND THEIR BATS

MATTHEW JOHN's bats are BULMER and WIMPY BAD BAT

JOSHUA RYAN's bats are SMOKY and SMALL BAD BAT

EMILY CHARLOTTE's bats are VESPER and MEDIUM BAD BAT

ANNABELLE SUE's bats are HULA and MAD BAD BAT

ADDISON CARTER's bats are MISTY and CRYSTAL

GABRIEL LOGAN's bat is PINKY

AKIHITO AKEMI's bat is SUKI

HANNAH BRIANNA's bats are BULMER and WINGY-THINGY

MR. SEEDS's bat is HOH-KAY otherwise known as BIG BAD BAT

ANOURA's bat is BAT

TUT-NUT's bat is MYSTACINA

PANA RANA's bat is NOCTILIO

KING MIMON's bat is WALLOP

ANTONINA VLADLENA's bat is SPUTNIK

HUI CHEN's bat is XIAO-XIAO

IA is the GREAT BAT OF EVENING

ABOUT THE AUTHOR

Anthony Barton lives in Canada by the sea. As he writes about Matthew John and Bulmer, little brown bats dart past him at sunset. The bats eat five or six hundred mosquitoes every hour, and consume half their weight in insects every night. After they have fed, the bats cluster in crevices to keep themselves warm. Anthony Barton has a website where you may read more stories about Matthew John and other bat riders of Yumi. The website is anthonybarton.com

NOW AVAILABLE

A Book for Boys and Girls
by the Same Author
Anthony Barton

The Yumi Trees

The Yumi Trees is the sequel
to *Bat Rider*. The mile-high Yumi trees
are in danger and Matthew John and his friends
must brave a tidal wave and make friends with the
oldest tree in the forest in their bid to save them.

One reviewer writes:

'A children's world is inevitably one built
around colossal changes and an unavoidable
"metamorphosis" as they grow up. Suddenly
they can do things themselves and parents
can be a bit embarrassing but deeply loved!
For your children, assuming they have read
all of the Matthew John adventures and
have drawn close to all the Bat Riders,
The Yumi Trees provides a powerful
new step forward in their lives.'

The Yumi Trees is available as a printed book
with illustrations by the author
from Amazon.com

FREE BAT RIDER SERIAL

An Audio Serial for Boys and Girls
by the Same Author
Anthony Barton

Bat Rider and the Cave of Oomba

Bat Rider and the Cave of Oomba is an eight-part serial.
Narration is by the author, with music, bat squeaks and production by
Siri Arnet. All eight episodes are free and may be heard at
Podiobooks.com

www.ingramcontent.com/pod-product-compliance
Lightning Source LLC
Chambersburg PA
CBHW060831120626
46557CB00001B/454